I0616830

Flurry the Bear

The Granted Wish

J.S. Skye

All characters featured in this novel, the distinctive names and likenesses thereof, and all related content are the sole property of J.S. Skye. No similarity between any of the names, characters, persons, and/or institutions in this book with those of any living or dead person or institution is intended, and any such similarity which may exist is purely coincidental.

The Granted Wish
(Flurry the Bear – Book 1)
Copyright © 2017 J.S. Skye
All rights reserved.
www.FlurryTheBear.com

Cover art by Luís Figueiredo, J.S. Skye, & Tony Washington

ISBN: 0692866744
ISBN-13: 978-0692866740

CONTENTS

CHAPTER 1
A MOTHER'S JOY

The stars vibrantly twinkled high above the snow-topped trees. The evening breeze was ever so gentle as it whirled about the chilly terrain. In a valley, enclosed by mountains, sat a cozy little village named Ursus.

The calm of the village made it effortless to hear the laughter of little teddy bear cubs. They scampered along the cobblestone path. "Hurry!" shouted one of the cubs, who had run out ahead of the others.

The cubs complied with the command of

their self-appointed leader and picked up the pace. They briskly passed by shops that had closed for the night and other plush bears that were headed home. Eventually they emerged beyond the boundaries of the village and arrived at a very large stone house that sat on the outskirts. The enormous home was breathtakingly beautiful, perched on a small hill across from a stone bridge that overlooked an icy brook.

Upon the threshold Christopher stood. He was a tall man in his early forties with a dark beard which sported some gray streaks Next to the man stood his lovely wife, Catherine. Her appearance was quite youthful. She had long, red hair and vibrant, green eyes. "Welcome! Welcome!" greeted the gentleman with his arms outstretched.

"Thank you, Mr. Kringle!" replied the cubs in unison. Catherine opened the door and escorted her visitors into a large room warmed by a fireplace. Once inside, the cubs were served many delectable and savory treats. It was the Christmas season, and that was the most cherished time of year for the little bear cubs. Their visit to the Kringle household was a tradition, and each of them looked forward to it every year.

As the plush bears nibbled on their cookies around the fireplace, Mrs. Kringle asked, "Who wants to hear a story?"

The cubs unanimously raised their paws and shouted, "Me!" or "I do!"

The Kringle couple laughed at how adorable the cubs were. Their energy and enthusiasm invigorated them. The missus then asked, "What story would you like me to read?"

One cub jumped to his feet and excitedly replied, "I want to hear a story about Flurry!" The other cubs glanced up with ecstatic faces – as if they had not considered that as an option.

"Yeah, me, too!" shouted another cub.

Before long, the room roared with cubs that wanted various stories, but they all related to Flurry in some manner. In fact, the versions of the stories were so numerous that Christopher realized that Flurry must have spun a few yarns of his own. So, the jolly fellow made a suggestion of his own "How about we read Flurry's very first tale?"

The cubs agreed, but were barely able to hold still. One cub spoke up. "May we hear the story about how he lost his tail?"

"Yeah!" shouted another cub.

A bit surprised by this, Christopher had to ask, "What do you mean?"

After only a brief moment he realized that he should have known better than to inquire. The room suddenly broke in chaos. The cubs shouted and argued over their wide array of answers.

"I heard he got it cut off by an evil pirate!" announced one of the cubs.

"Nuh uh! He said it was bitten off by a dinosaur!" shouted another.

"No! You're both wrong! He told me a monster ripped it off!" chimed a third.

The room was saturated in arguments over what was really the true story about Flurry's absent tail. Christopher and his wife exchanged exasperated glances – little did they know that Flurry's tail was so important. The man of the house decided to put an end to the squabbles. "Quiet! Quiet! Quiet down, please!" he pleaded with his arms raised.

The cubs all took their seats and hushed down. Their little eyes looked up at Mr. Kringle with expectancy. Mrs. Kringle was pleasantly surprised to see such obedience.

About this time, there was a knock at the door. "I wonder who that could be," the lady of the house remarked to herself. Catherine approached the door and opened it to reveal another young lady. She was dressed in knee-high leather boots and a black leather jacket. The visitor had long, straight hair, and both her eyes and her locks were brown. Her complexion was soft, and she had two black stripes painted across her face at her eye level.

"Welcome! It's been a long time!" Mrs. Kringle was clearly delighted with her visitor. The ladies shared a brief embrace. Catherine continued. "Come in! We were just about to have story time with the cubs. Would you like to join us?"

"Of course! Thank you," answered the visitor.

"What brings you this far north?"

Mrs. Kringle's company replied, "I'm here to see Yudel."

"Yudel?" Catherine paused. She shot a glance at her husband. Christopher responded with a shrug. She turned back and continued. "I haven't seen him in quite a while! Is he supposed to be coming here, too?"

"Yes. I must've made better time than I thought."

Mrs. Kringle smiled, turned to her adorable audience, and announced, "Cubs, this is Nomi. She's an old friend of ours."

"Is she going to read to us?" asked one of the bears.

The adults chuckled, and then Nomi responded, "Sure! I'd be honored to read you a story." She looked to the Kringles and asked, "What story shall I read to them?"

Mrs. Kringle took an ornate blue book from her husband's lap and handed it to Nomi.

Nomi accepted the book and sat down in a large, comfy seat by the fire. She opened the book, turned to the first page, and read the title, "The Granted Wish."

The faces of the cubs intently turned to Nomi. Very little could break them free from her words. Some cubs sat there with half eaten cookies, because nothing else mattered to them but the knowledge of Flurry's beginning. Nomi turned the page and began to read.

*****

Once upon a time, there was a quaint, little village named Ursus. This small settlement sat in the cold, blustery land of Mezarim, but many referred to it as the North Pole. This village was home to a community of teddy bears. Among the houses of these fuzzy neighbors was a beige-colored dwelling with a brown roof and a blue front door. Behind the windows were curtains that matched the hue of the front entrance. It was a warm, comfortable house with a chimney, which battled the chilly temperature of the tundra. Under its roof lived a lovely teddy bear couple known to everyone as the Snow family.

This cute couple was well-loved by the entire community. Mr. Snow was of a lighter shade of brown, almost the hue of caramel. In contrast to his fur, he wore a tiny blue bow tie with two embroidered snowflakes upon it. These snowflakes were the Snow family's crest.

Other members of the Snow family also bore their family seal on articles of their own clothing. In fact, each of the teddy bear families wore their own family's symbol on their attire somewhere.

Other than a bow tie, Mr. Snow often wore his utility belt as though it were one of his garments. He did this even on his days off from work. Mr. Snow often said, "You never know when this might come in handy." He was renowned throughout Ursus for his expert carpentry skills.

His wife had fur as white as snow – how fitting that her married name was Snow! She wore a blue dress with pink hearts at the fringe, and a blue bow adorned the top of her head. The pink hearts matched her little pink nose, which made her look all the more adorable. Mr. and Mrs. Snow were a young couple, and they were tremendously happy together. They had been married for many years, but they did not have any cubs of their own.

It was not that Mr. and Mrs. Snow did not want a cub to call their own, but the missus assumed that it would be too much to ask for such a large favor from Christopher Kringle. Christopher was the one who granted life to all of the teddy bears, but he could only do this by the will and help of the Great King, who gave him this ability to work such a miracle. Without the Great King's gift, it would be impossible for a plush bear to come to life.

Christopher would have granted Mr. and Mrs. Snow's desire for a cub, if only they had asked. The Snow couple was very polite and respectful. They avoided any circumstance that made them feel as though they had intruded on or inconvenienced anyone.

Every Christmas Eve, Christopher would grant a wish to one lucky citizen from Ursus – assuming that it was within his power to grant. All of the villagers' names were placed into a big glass jar for Christopher to reach into and draw out a name at random.

The name-drawing always took place the morning of Christmas Eve. This was done so that the lucky winner would have time to plan what they would ask of Christopher later that night.

At midnight on Christmas Eve, all of the bear community would gather at the town center and celebrate the granting of one wish before Christopher went out to make his rounds in the neighboring human city of Polaris.

Up until now, neither Mr. nor Mrs. Snow had ever had their names drawn. However, this day things would be different.

It was the morning of Christmas Eve, and it seemed like any other day – at least for a northerner. Being so far north, it remained dark the entire day. Only in the summer did they have entire days of sunlight.

This morning, though still dark, Mr. Snow headed off to work as he did every weekday. Mrs. Snow made her husband a sack lunch to take with him, but he was well on his way down the cobblestone path before she noticed that he had left it behind.

It was an easy thing to forget on a day like this. Christmas Eve was always an exciting time. Mr. Snow, being a carpenter, had a lot of work to do. His skills with wood made him the ideal candidate to carve out hand-crafted toys. He found considerable joy in the knowledge that his creations would be loved by children and cubs all over his world and ours. Mrs. Snow chased after her husband and called out to him, "Honey! You forgot your lunch!"

"Why thank you, my dear! What would I do without you?" Mr. Snow replied.

Mrs. Snow gave him a kiss on the cheek and handed him the brown paper bag. "Goodbye! Have a good day! I love you!" she shouted to him and waved.

With a big smile on his face, Mr. Snow waved back and replied, "I love you, too!"

Mrs. Snow returned to the house and shut the door behind her. She gazed out from the window and watched her husband walk to work.

After her spouse had faded off into the distance, Mrs. Snow turned from the window and to her task at hand. Today, she had a considerable amount of house cleaning to do. She planned to have guests over later and wanted the house to be presentable.

Mrs. Snow had not cleaned for more than a few minutes when there was a knock at the door. "That's odd," she said to herself. "I'm not expecting anyone this early."

She gracefully skipped over to the door, anxious to see who it might be. She peeked through the peephole, and saw her brother-in-law Chip's wife. Her name was Bubbles, and she was a delightfully energetic bear. Bubbles always had a way with the cubs, due to such a cheerful personality.

Mrs. Snow opened the door and saw the excited look on her sister-in-law's face. Bubbles' yellow fur accented her radiant demeanor.

Bubbles rushed into the house and gave Mrs. Snow a big hug. Surprised, Mrs. Snow asked, "Wow! What's that for?"

Equally surprised, Bubbles replied, "You don't know? Haven't you heard the news? You were chosen in the lottery this morning. You get to make a wish tonight. It's so exciting!"

Mrs. Snow did not respond. In fact, she did not know what to say. It felt like a dream, and she was afraid that someone might wake her up at any moment. She stood motionless, as if she were made from stone. A tear trickled down her cheek.

Bubbles continued on, "This is great! Now you can finally be a mom! I'll be an aunt! Then your cub and my cubs can play together, and …"

Before Bubbles could finish, Mrs. Snow realized that she had a very limited amount of time before she would need to make her wish. In a panic, she stopped Bubbles mid-sentence. "Oh my! I have to go! I need to make preparations!"

Mrs. Snow bolted out the door. After a few steps, she realized what she had done.

Mrs. Snow turned around and ran back up to her friend and family member. "I'm so sorry, but I have to go. Thank you for telling me. I'll see you tonight, right?" Mrs. Snow gave Bubbles a hug, waved goodbye, and ran off again.

The trip to the town center seemed to take but mere moments. Mrs. Snow could think of nothing else than what she had to do. She rushed into a little shop, out of breath. "Well, hello there," came the storekeeper's greeting. He was about a foot taller than Mrs. Snow, and he had dark brown fur, a forest green apron, and bifocals.

Mrs. Snow gasped for breath. She attempted to communicate while she panted. With broken speech she replied, "Hello ... Do you have white ... fur that I ... could purchase from you?"

The storekeeper looked at her with intrigue. He wondered what her rush was, but he was too polite to inquire. "Well, let's take a look. I don't see why I wouldn't. I try to keep my shop fully stocked at all times."

The storekeeper walked over to a shelf which contained stacks of fur. He rummaged through the different types and colors. "I have brown, green, black, blue, pink, and … Aha! White!"

"Oh, thank you so much!" Mrs. Snow replied with a broken voice. She, once again, neared having tears of joy. "How much do I owe you?"

"Well, your husband is a good friend and since it's 'that' time of year, consider it a gift. I can see how much it means to you, and your joy is enough of a payment for me."

For the second time that morning, Mrs. Snow found herself speechless. "I don't know what to say. Thank you so much! If there's anything I can do for you …"

"You already have," the storekeeper replied with a smile, and walked back to the counter.

"Thank you, again! I won't ever forget this!" Mrs. Snow rushed out the door, and nearly tripped at the threshold as she hurried home.

Throughout the hours that followed, the missus worked diligently on her special project. Before long, she realized that her day had come and gone in a pinch. Evening fast approached.

Mr. Snow arrived at his home. He opened the door to enter. He expected to find the place to be in tip top condition, but he noticed that the house had not been cleaned at all. It was uncommon for Mrs. Snow not to be prepared for company. He looked to his left, and over by the fireplace he saw something he did not intend to find.

Mrs. Snow sat on their strawberry-colored couch with a little ball of white fur in her arms. The fireplace was lit, and a cup of tea sat upon the coffee table next to her. She leaned against the arm of the couch for support. It was clear to her husband that she had been hard at work on what he beheld in her arms.

Mr. Snow closed the front door and approached the side of the couch. He was eager to get a closer look at what his wife cuddled. Wrapped in a blue blanket was an adorable bear cub. The bear had deep black eyes, a brown nose, and fur whiter than snow. Mr. Snow could see a resemblance to his wife in the little cub. At his spouse's feet sat a partially finished blue scarf. She had laid it on the cushion adjacent to her.

Mr. Snow peered down at the darling cub and said, "He's quite adorable. He has your fur."

"He has your eyes," replied his wife.

"What should we name him?" Mr. Snow asked. He put his arm around his wife and reached out with one paw to pull the blanket away from the baby bear's face.

"Well, I was thinking of naming him Flurry. His fur is certainly as white, if not whiter, than snow. He's also very small, like a little snowflake. What do you think?"

Mr. Snow noticed the sparkle in her eyes. He nodded in agreement and said, "Flurry it is! That's a fine name for my firstborn son."

Mr. Snow bent down and gave each of them a kiss on the cheek. "You relax. I'll prepare the house for our guests."

"Okay. I'll finish his scarf, and then help out with whatever's left to do," Mrs. Snow added.

When Mrs. Snow put the completed scarf on her cub, a look of horror came across her face. She realized that she had somehow forgotten something very important. She gently laid the baby bear in the basket on the couch, and then rushed out of the house.

In her haste, she forgot to grab her coat, close the door, or even inform her husband where she was going. She ran as fast as her legs would take her. Though she traveled the same route she had taken that morning, this trip dragged on for what she would have described as an eternity.

Just as before, she arrived at the shop out of breath. She gasped for air. The lady bear looked up and saw the sign on the door which read: "Closed." Mrs. Snow fell to her knees and wept bitterly.

The storekeeper was still inside. He had cleaned up for the night, and was about to turn out the lights when he heard a strange sound from beyond the front door. He listened closely and recognized the sound of mournful weeping. He opened the door and found Mrs. Snow on her knees. She knelt in the middle of what would have been a puddle of water, had it not become a sheet of ice.

"Oh dear! How long have you been out here?" the storekeeper asked.

"I don't know," she sobbed.

"Well, what's the matter?"

"I ran out of fur to finish my son, and it's only a few hours until midnight."

"Well, don't give up yet. Let's take a look at what I have. Here, come in out of the cold." The storekeeper held the door for her and waved her inside. He grabbed a blanket and laid it over her shoulders. "Here, this should warm you up a bit while I look."

The storekeeper dug around and checked every shelf, cabinet, and drawer. "Hmmm … I don't seem to have any more white fur. I have an off-white color you could use. Would that be okay?"

Mrs. Snow shook her head in disbelief. Her vision of a perfect son had been shattered.

"I'll be putting in an order for some more. It should be here in about a week."

Mrs. Snow broke down again. Her tears

ran down her ivory fur. She buried her face in her paws. "You don't understand, I need it tonight, or my son won't be completed in time for the gathering."

"There, there, it's not the end of the world. Ask Mr. Kringle. I'm sure he can make some sort of allowance for you." The storekeeper rubbed her back and attempted to console her.

"I couldn't ask that of him. It's okay. I should go now. Thank you for the blanket and for trying to help me. Merry Christmas!" She returned the blanket to the storekeeper, and went outside to journey back home. This time her trip was vastly different than before. Each footstep was heavy, and it took every ounce of her strength to move forward. She walked so slowly that it was very late in the night by the time she had returned home. All of her guests had come and gone in her absence.

When she reached the front door, Mr. Snow saw her from the window. He rushed out to her with an extra coat. "Dear, where have you been? Our guests and I have been so worried about you. Nobody knew where you were. Are you okay?" Mrs. Snow could not answer. She just cried and sniffled. Mr. Snow brought her inside and sat her down by the fireplace. He then brought her some tissues for her nose and wiped her tears away. "What is it, Darling? You can tell me."

In between her sobs she answered, "I failed! I failed you, I failed myself, and most importantly I failed Flurry!"

"Now, now, what's gotten into you? Why do you feel this way?" asked her husband.

She quickly responded in a raised tone, "Because! Don't you see? It's almost midnight, and our son isn't finished! I forgot to give him a tail, and the shopkeeper is all out of white fur. I also ..."

Before she could finish her rant, her husband chuckled, rubbed her back, and interjected. "Sweetie! He's perfect just as he is! He doesn't need to have a tail to be our son. You've created the finest and cutest teddy bear the world has ever seen. You should be proud. I'm certainly proud of you, and I'm proud to have Flurry as my son, tail or no tail."

Mrs. Snow's face lit up. "Really?" she sobbed.

"Of course!" reassured her husband. Mr. Snow got up, walked over to the basket, scooped the cub into his arms, and placed the tiny bear into the soon-to-be mother's embrace. "Here! Hold him while I help you with the door. You don't want to be late for your wish, do you?"

A smile came upon her face. She got up, kissed her husband on the cheek, and said, "I love you, my big snuggle bear." Mr. Snow closed the door behind them, and off they went to see Christopher Kringle.

When they arrived at the town center, they could see the entire body of villagers gathered together. Christopher himself was already there and anxiously awaited their arrival.

"I was beginning to think you weren't going to show up," Christopher commented with a chuckle. "And what have we here? Let me see this handsome fellow." Christopher squatted down and held out his arms for the cub. Mrs. Snow put the little bear safely in the man's grasp.

Christopher examined the baby bear closely, and then looked back at Mr. and Mrs. Snow. "You know, this is the cutest, most adorable teddy bear I've ever seen! Mrs. Snow, you've outdone yourself with your craftsmanship. Your work is deserving of the wish you've wanted me to grant for so long."

"How have you known what my wish has been for so long? I've not told you before." Mrs. Snow was quite surprised Mr. Kringle would know such a thing.

Christopher stood up and chuckled. "My dear! Everyone knows how much you've wanted your own cub, and tonight I'm going to grant you that very wish. So tell me, my dear, what may I call this youngster?"

In unison, Mr. and Mrs. Snow both replied, "His name is Flurry."

Christopher could see how proud they were of their new boy. He crouched back down, peered into the eyes of the little cub, and whispered in the baby bear's ear. "Flurry! Flurry! Wake up. Your parents are here to see you." Mr. and Mrs. Snow watched. Flurry blinked his eyes for the first time, took in a breath of air, and said, "San'ta"?

Christopher's mouth fell open. He had been caught off guard. There was an extended moment of silence. Christopher had not expected Flurry to speak so soon, nor did he know how Flurry could have possibly known the meaning of the word "San'ta". *Perhaps this is simply some form of baby talk?* he wondered to himself.

Christopher reasoned that it could not possibly be that Flurry knew how to say "father" in Polarin – the dialect of Mezarim. Christopher cleared his throat and said, "No, my name is Christopher." The man did not expect that the cub would understand his speech.

Flurry replied, "Santa!" and clutched Christopher around the neck with a loving hug. Amusement broke out among the crowd. The villagers giggled. Christopher also chuckled at how adorable Flurry was.

Christopher stood up and held Flurry above his head for the entire village to see. Everyone cheered. Mr. Snow put his arm around his wife. She cried tears of joy. Mr. Snow could barely contain his own emotions.

As he held Flurry up in the air,

Christopher announced, "Behold! I give you Flurry Snow! May Flurry and his family be ever blessed! Let blessings also be upon all who meet Flurry, for I know a blessing has been bestowed upon me!"

Christopher walked over to Mr. and Mrs. Snow, put Flurry into his mother's arms, and said, "Flurry, these are your parents. Be good to them, for they love you very much." Flurry looked up at them and said, "Mama? Papa? I love you!" They both hugged him, and the entire village shouted with joy.

Christopher was perplexed by the cub's ability to not only speak, but to speak both Polarin and English. This event was unprecedented. Christopher took note of this and kept it in the back of his mind. There was something special about this cub that was unlike any that had come before him.

Christopher pulled Mr. Snow aside and remarked, "You know, he's surprisingly smart, more so than usual. He has a rare and special gift. Take good care of him."

"I most certainly will," Mr. Snow proudly responded.

Christopher turned to Mrs. Snow and spoke softly in her ear. "I can see that he looks a bit like you, but I also noticed he has an uncanny resemblance to the statue. I assume this isn't a coincidence?"

The statue Christopher referred to was in the center of Ursus, just a stone's throw from where he currently stood. It depicted a hero that had saved the first teddy bear village from an evil enemy thousands of years ago. Mrs. Snow answered him and said, "Yes, a little bit. It was certainly an inspiration. I hope my son will follow in the footsteps of such greatness."

"Indeed he will! I foresee it," Christopher confidently replied.

The band commenced with cheerful music, confetti fell from above, and the teddy bears danced and celebrated all throughout the town. In the midst of the commotion, Mr. and Mrs. Snow lost sight of Christopher. The last thing they remembered was when Christopher chuckled to himself and said, "Well, I'm off. I can't delay too long or the children won't be getting any gifts this year."

Wherever Christopher disappeared to, Mr. and Mrs. Snow did not know. They had been too focused on their newborn son to be able to take notice of anything else. They were immeasurably happy that their dream had finally been realized. The Snow couple looked down at the shiny little eyes that gazed back up at them. They finally got their wish. They now had a son.

*****

CHAPTER 2
MISUNDERSTOOD

"Wait a minute! That's not how it happened!" shouted an outraged cub. His outburst disrupted the mood. The other cubs snapped out of the world they pictured in their heads.

Nomi closed the book, but kept the page marked with her finger.

Soon the other bears argued about the validity of Nomi's story. It did not line up with what Flurry had told them.

Christopher held up his hands to calm the cubs down. "I'm sorry if this isn't what you heard from Flurry, but this really is the truth."

"So he never had a tail?" asked another of the young bears.

"That's correct," Christopher replied.

"No, that doesn't sound right," yet another chimed in.

Mrs. Kringle gave her husband a look that he knew all too well. He cleared his throat and continued. "Do you want to hear the rest of the story, or do you want to all go home and be put to bed?"

The cubs were instantly seated and insisted that Nomi continue the story. The lady smiled and opened to the next chapter.

*****

The sheer joy and excitement Mr. and Mrs. Snow felt was immeasurable. They spent every available moment with their son. As often as time would allow, they took Flurry outdoors and built snowbears, competed in snowball fights, and sledded down the steep hills all around Ursus. Flurry loved to play, and everywhere he went cheer spread.

It was difficult for anyone in Ursus to know how much time had passed while Flurry resided at the North Pole. However, the amount of time that had gone by was not important. The most crucial thing was how Flurry would become what he was destined to be.

As time proved, Flurry was a well-behaved little bear – for the most part. However, he managed to get himself into trouble every now and then. He often went to Mrs. Daybear's house to recruit his buddy, Sunny. Together, the boys embarked on adventures right there in their backyard – you would be surprised what kind of secrets wait to be discovered in your own yard.

At the schoolhouse, Flurry often snuck off with Sunny to play. It was not done out of defiance to authority, nor was it intentional mischief. Flurry was a cub, and he was easily influenced by the promise of adventure – besides, what child would not?

One particular school day, Flurry stared out the window and watched the snow elegantly drift down onto the tree branches. The moon made the snowflakes sparkle in her light. As the lunar rays cast their cool glow on Flurry's face, he dreamed away.

Flurry sat at his desk, unaware of anything the teacher had said to him. In his fantasies of great adventures, which beckoned to him from the distant horizon, her words began to break through as if from another world.

"Flurry!" sounded the voice of his school teacher. The cub remained in that happy place and did not hear his name being called. "Flurry!" she shouted again. One final time the instructor bellowed, "Flurry!"

The cub jumped up with a start, and answered, "I didn't do it!"

The classroom giggled. Flurry tried to get his bearings straight.

"No, I called on you to answer the

question. What starts with the letter T?"

"Toothpaste?" Flurry answered uneasily. His voice indicated that he was unsure of himself. He had no idea what she had last spoken about. The classroom burst into laughter.

"Flurry! Were you paying attention at all? Toothpaste isn't a name of an animal!" The teacher shook her head and approached Flurry's desk. She stood over Flurry and peered down at him through her bifocals.

"It could be!" he shouted. When he saw that she was not convinced, he continued in a lower octave. "Well, if someone had a pet and named it Toothpaste." Flurry looked up and grinned uneasily. If Flurry could have made a halo appear above his head, he would have.

The instructor glared at the boy cub with

disapproval. Flurry looked up at the gray furry figure which stood over him. The cub's eyes watered. "I'm sorry," Flurry cried.

"Sorry isn't good enough! You need to start paying attention! I'm trying to teach the alphabet, and you're off in your own little world! Should I write a letter to your parents?"

"Which letter?" Flurry asked. "You have twenty-six of them to choose from." Flurry misunderstood her meaning, but his statement came across as sarcasm.

"Oh! I see how it is. You want to be a wise guy, eh? First, it was Drizzle. Now, it's you, too? So be it! I'll write an extensive letter to your parents, and inform them of what a poor student you've been." The instructor huffed as if she were a steam engine. She quickly spun around, and marched back to her desk in front of the classroom.

"Oh no! Please don't! I'll do anything! I'll pay attention from now on, I promise!" Before Flurry could get an answer from his instructor, the bell rang.

"You're all dismissed," she informed the class.

Flurry quickly slipped out from his chair and raced toward the door. He had only just escaped when Sunny showed up.

"Hey, Flurry!" Sunny called out to Flurry from down the long hallway.

Flurry waved back. "Hello!"

Sunny's yellow fur brightened Flurry's mood. "Flurry! I thought of something fun we can do!"

"What's that?" Flurry excitedly replied.

"There's this amazing tree out in front of our houses. We should climb it and see who can get to the top the quickest."

"I don't know. That sounds fun, but my mama and papa might not like that. They don't think it's safe to climb trees," Flurry replied with a discouraged tone to his voice.

"Come on! Live a little! Nobody will know." Sunny tried to sound convincing. He pulled his red handkerchief up over his face. "See! You can't even tell who I am, can you?"

Flurry was not convinced, but he gave in just the same. "Oh, okay. Only for a little bit, and then I need to get home or my mama will be worried about me." Then, a hint of caution crept back in as Flurry asked, "Just promise me we won't climb too high, okay?"

"Sure! I promise!" Sunny sounded sincere, so Flurry joined him and they rushed off on their adventure. Deep down, Flurry knew that he could not trust Sunny at his word. However, Sunny told Flurry what he wanted to hear.

Their choice tree was very close to both of their homes. They arrived at the tree and remained still for a moment. The boys contemplated their method for ascending the giant towering over them. It was clear that getting to the first branch was going to be their biggest challenge – after all, they were only teddy bear cubs, and they were not very tall. Sunny, after he had stacked up some rocks, gave Flurry a boost. In return, Flurry pulled Sunny up into the tree with him.

Flurry used his scarf to make up for the lack of reach that he needed.

"I'll race you to the top branch," Sunny challenged.

"You're on!" Flurry exclaimed. Before he made a move, Flurry took a peek out from the branches and realized how high up they were. He swallowed hard, closed his eyes, and reached for the first of many branches.

Flurry's fear eventually subsided. The boys giggled and tried to outmaneuver each other. However, Flurry and Sunny's fun screeched to a halt when they heard a fur-curling scream. "Sunny! Get down from there this instant! How many times have I told you to stop climbing trees?"

Sunny poked his head out from the branches and saw that his mother stood at

47

the base of the tree with her paws at her hips.

Sunny pulled his head back in, and with a startled voice whispered to Flurry, "It's my mom! I'm in so much trouble! I have to go now. Bye!"

Flurry whispered back, "Okay, goodbye!" Flurry stuck his head out, and saw Sunny's angry mother. She glared back at him. "Oh! I see what's going on here! This is your fault, isn't it?" she sternly addressed Flurry.

"No, it isn't, I promise!" Flurry attempted to defend himself.

"I'll hear no more of it! You're a bad influence on my boy! I don't want you playing with him anymore!"

"Mother, Flurry didn't do anything. I asked him to come with me." Sunny interjected.

Sunny's mother would not accept it. "You don't need to make excuses for him. Before you met Flurry, you didn't get in as much trouble as you do now. It's obvious that he has a negative effect on you. It comes from poor upbringing. In the end, his parents are to blame. Come on, let's go home!"

Before she had walked too far from the tree, she looked back and shouted, "As for you! I have half a mind to have a little chat with your parents, too! Maybe they'll finally give you some much-needed discipline!"

"No, Mrs. Daybear! Please!" Flurry pleaded, but his words fell on deaf ears.

Flurry sat in the tree and sulked. He wondered why he was so misunderstood by others. How could he be blamed for something that was not even his idea? He

49

realized that he should have just said no.

It suddenly dawned on Flurry that his parents would be home soon. He quickly navigated the branches, but his haste did not prepare him for the patch of ice at the lowest branch. Before Flurry knew what happened, his foot gave way, and he fell from the tree.

Luckily, Flurry had two things going for him. First of all, there was a snow drift to cushion his fall. Secondly, he was a teddy bear. Teddy bears do not have to worry about getting hurt in the same manner that a real bear would.

Flurry impacted the snow. A white cloud of flakes swirled up around him. Flurry got up and brushed off the snow, shook his head, and ran for home.

The distance from the tree to his house was not far, but Flurry sat up in the tree far longer than he realized. The moon was much higher in the sky now. To Flurry's horror, Mrs. Daybear was already at the door of his home. She spoke loudly to his mother, and waved her arms demonstratively.

Flurry arrived and squeezed in between the door frame and Mrs. Daybear's left leg. Flurry looked back at her from inside only to be met with an angry scowl.

At school, many of the other cubs often joked about Mrs. Daybear. They liked to say she permanently had a disgruntled look on her face, and that she did not know how to smile. Flurry thought about it and realized he was unable to think of a single moment when Mrs. Daybear did not look upset.

Poor Mrs. Daybear, maybe she just needs a hug, Flurry thought to himself. Before he

51

could dwell on the subject any longer, Flurry was brought back to the moment at hand.

He heard his mother say goodbye, followed with, "Okay, I'll look into it. Thank you." The door clicked shut, and Mrs. Snow turned to face her son. Strangely, she did not appear the way Flurry had anticipated. Instead of having a look of anger, she appeared to be sad.

Tears formed in his mother's eyes. "Flurry, I don't know what to say to you right now. Do you know how dangerous that was? What if something bad had happened to you? You're my only son." As she wept, Flurry felt tremendous guilt. He had not thought about how his actions would affect her or anyone else but himself.

"I'm sorry, Mama!" Flurry cuddled up against his mother after she sat down on the couch.

Later that evening, Mr. Snow came home and found his wife and son huddled together on the couch. While she stroked Flurry's head, Mrs. Snow looked up at her husband with a concerned look in her eyes. Mr. Snow knew this expression well. "What is it?" he asked with hesitation in his voice.

She replied, "Mrs. Daybear came to see me today. She was angry at Flurry, and blamed him for getting her son to climb trees with him."

After he patiently listened to his wife's entire account of events, Flurry's father asked his son, "Is this true?"

"I did climb a tree with Sunny, but it was his idea. I didn't want to, but …"

Before Flurry could finish, his father

spoke over him. "Flurry, what are we going to do with you? You know climbing trees isn't safe, don't you?"

"Yes, Papa, I know." Flurry dropped his gaze. He stared at the floor with regret for how foolish he had been.

"Then why do you continue to do it?" asked the cub's father.

"I don't know, maybe because it's fun?" Flurry answered.

That was not the response Flurry's parents wanted to hear. Suddenly, both his mother and father were angry. His father stood with his paws on his hips. "Because it's fun? Because it's fun? Go to your room!" shouted Mr. Snow. Flurry rushed off to his bedroom. Tears trickled down his furry cheeks.

Mr. Snow sat down in his chair. The look

on his face conveyed deep reflection. He thought about what he should do to properly discipline his son.

"What are we going to do with him?" Mr. Snow asked his wife. He looked over at her and saw that she was in tears again.

Mrs. Snow came and stood next to her husband's chair and sobbed, "I'm not sure. Scolding him doesn't seem to work. Maybe we should ground him? We could forbid him from playing outside until he can learn to obey us." Mrs. Snow rubbed her husband's arm to comfort him. She hoped that it would reassure him that her idea would work. It broke her heart to know that Flurry had such a difficult time – seeing Flurry cry could melt the hardest of hearts.

"Well, you know that I work during the

day. Will you be able to keep your eye on him all day long? That could be a tall order!"

Mrs. Snow reassured her husband. "I'm sure I'll be fine." Then she joked, "I do have eyes in the back of my head."

The next day, Flurry sat at the front window and watched the other cubs play outside. The others had fun outside in the snow while Flurry was confined to the prison of his own home. The day dragged on. He tried numerous projects to keep himself occupied, but to no avail. Flurry longed to be free.

"I'm so bored!" he shouted. Flurry hopped down from the windowsill, grabbed his ball, and bounced it around. No sooner had he begun to play with it than it bounced off of the wall and collided with his mother's vase. The flowers tumbled from the table. Flurry cringed as the ceramic décor shattered into numerous fragments. The entire event unfolded in slow motion. The commotion startled Flurry so much that he dove under the couch for cover.

When Flurry peeked out and saw the broken shards of pottery and dirt strewn across the floor, he exclaimed, "Uh oh!" Flurry realized that he may not see the outside world for a very long time.

Fast-paced footsteps were heard. Flurry's mother rushed into the room. "Flurry! What was that? Are you okay?" When Mrs. Snow saw the mess, she responded, "Oh, Flurry! What did you do?"

The cub climbed out from under the couch. A puddle of tears rested upon the floor where he had concealed himself. The bear ran and embraced his mother and wept. "I'm sorry, Mama! I didn't mean to! I was bored. I wanted to play with my ball, and it accidentally hit the vase. I didn't mean to! I'm sorry!"

Mrs. Snow saw her boy's adorable little face all drenched with tears, and her heart melted. "Oh, my little dear, come here." Flurry squeezed tighter as she continued to embrace and comfort him.

Mrs. Snow took a seat on the couch and placed her son on her lap. She listened to Flurry continue. "I don't mean to get into trouble, Mama. Honest! I feel like I'm always disappointing you and Papa. I'm so sorry!" He sobbed even more. Flurry now had a tear soaked scarf in addition to his tear soaked fur.

She attempted to comfort her son while he sat on her lap. "It's okay, my sweetheart. Accidents happen. I have an idea! Why don't you go to the grocery store and pick up some items for your mother while I clean up the mess, and start preparing dinner? That way you can get out of the house for a little bit. Does that sound okay to you?"

"Uh huh," her boy sobbed and wiped the tears away from his eyes.

"Good! Now go get ready, and I'll make a list."

Flurry hopped down from his mother's lap and quickly ran off to his room. He returned very shortly after his mother had finished the grocery list. However, Flurry ran right past her and bolted out the door. He was so happy he was free from the house

59

that he forgot what he was going out for in the first place.

Before he got too far away from the threshold, his mother cleared her throat. "Aren't you forgetting something?" she asked.

"Oh yeah!" Flurry exclaimed. He ran back in and hugged his mother. "I love you, Mama! Okay, goodbye!" He returned to his mission, and headed straight for the door again.

Amused, Mrs. Snow chuckled and said, "Yes, that was very sweet of you, but that wasn't what I meant. Aren't you forgetting something else? I'll give you a hint. It's a four letter word that starts with an L, and ends with a T."

Flurry looked back and saw his mother wave a piece of paper in her paw. "Oh yeah!

Sorry!" Flurry rushed back up to his mother and snatched the list from her grip.

Flurry called out, "Okay, goodbye!" and rushed out the door. Just as before, Flurry darted off in a hurry. He only turned for a moment to wave to his mother.

Flurry's mother waved back. She had a proud smile upon her face. She was amused at just how adorable her son could be. Then suddenly she thought to herself, *I hope he doesn't get into any more trouble while he's out.*

On the way to the shop, Flurry imagined what it would be like to purchase groceries like the grownups do. He pictured how happy his mother and how proud his father would be. Flurry did not even notice the other cubs that played in the snow. He was on a mission of the utmost importance, and nothing could distract him.

Flurry arrived at the shop. Being so small, he had to wait outside for an older bear to come out, which allowed him to slip in. Once inside, Flurry felt a sense of awe, for the store was filled with so many goodies, many of which were beyond his reach. Flurry had been to the grocery store many times with his parents, but this was his first time to be there on his own. He felt so proud. He was just like one of the grownups now.

On his way through the store, a stack of honey jars caught his attention. "Oooh!" Flurry exclaimed. He was mesmerized by the sheer number of them. They towered over the cub. Flurry looked at his list. "Mama didn't put honey on the list, but I'm sure she'll be happy if I bring one home for her. It'll be a gift to show her how much I love her."

Without hesitation, Flurry reached for one of the honey jars at the bottom of the stack and removed it. Flurry was not sure what happened next, because it happened so quickly. One moment Flurry was grocery shopping, and the next moment there were broken jars of honey spilled all over him and the floor. The storekeeper was beyond angry. The other shoppers stood by and stared at the cub. Flurry felt humiliated. The cub cried and rushed out of the store as quickly as possible.

Flurry ran home as fast as his little legs would take him. He entered the house and rushed up to his mother. The boy cried his eyes out. "Mama! Mama! I was … I … I wanted … I wanted to do something nice for you … and then the honey fell … and then everyone got angry … and then …" Between Flurry's sniffles, it was like trying to decipher a code. Mrs. Snow could tell something went horribly wrong and that it involved honey, since Flurry was covered in it.

"Flurry, calm down! I tell you what, go get the bathtub ready, and I'll be in to give you a bath in just a moment."

"Okay," Flurry answered. He shuffled away and sniffled while he rubbed his eyes.

Before long, Mrs. Snow entered the bathroom to help Flurry get cleaned up. She had just finished up when she heard voices outside on the sidewalk. She peeked out from a window and saw the grocery store owner and her husband in conversation. She could faintly make out the storekeeper's words, "You're a good bear, Mr. Snow, but your cub needs some discipline."

After their talk, Mr. Snow came in the front door and turned back to bid goodnight to the storekeeper. Flurry heard the door close and immediately submersed himself in the tub water.

"Now, Sweetie, don't be like that," his mother pleaded with him and lifted him back up by his arm. Flurry cringed at the sound of his father's footsteps. He heard them grow louder with each step up the stairway. In haste, Flurry gathered all of the soap bubbles from his bath and heaped them up over his head to disguise himself as a pile of suds. He had hoped that it would fool his

65

father into thinking that Flurry was not there.

There was a light knock at the bathroom door. "Where is he?" Mr. Snow asked.

Mrs. Snow rushed to the door, slipped out into the hallway, and closed the bathroom door behind her. "Now, honey, Flurry has had a rough day. I'll handle it. All I want to know is how bad it was."

"Well, the storekeeper owed me some favors from when I fixed up his shop last winter, so we called it even. I offered to have Flurry sent over to clean up the mess for him, but he insisted that I not let Flurry get anywhere near his shop. I think he's afraid that Flurry will find more trouble to get himself into."

Mrs. Snow's countenance fell. "Poor little guy. He has a big heart, and he means well. I wonder what we can do to keep him out of trouble."

"Hmmm …" Mr. Snow placed his paw upon his chin and thought about the matter. "Maybe we should bring this to Chris," Mr. Snow suggested. "Yes, I think I'll take him to Chris's house tomorrow, and see what he suggests." Mrs. Snow agreed with and embraced her husband.

With the matter settled, Mr. Snow called it a night. Mrs. Snow attended to Flurry's bath and fixed a late night treat for her boy. After she tucked Flurry in, she read him a short bedtime story. Then, it was off to bed for everyone in the Snow household.

Before she left, Mrs. Snow gave her boy a hug and kissed him on the cheek. She stroked the tuft of fur on his forehead and said to him, "Don't be sad, my darling, everything will work out. Now get some rest; you have a big day ahead of you tomorrow. Who knows? Maybe there'll be a surprise, too."

"Oooh! I love surprises! What is it, Mama?" Flurry excitedly asked.

"Now, now, it's time for bed. Sleep well, and I'll see my sweetie when he wakes up. I love you," his mother said and then turned out the light.

"I love you, too! Okay, goodnight!" Flurry pulled the warm blanket up to his chin. Flurry felt comforted. He wondered what tomorrow would bring. Before long, he was asleep. He dreamed of tasty treats, and epic adventures.

CHAPTER 3
MR. KRINGLE

The following morning had arrived. Flurry sat up in his bed and rubbed his eyes. Despite the darkness just beyond the walls of his room, it was a new morning: a fresh start. Flurry lingered among the sheets until he heard something that he had not expected.

From the foot of the steps, Flurry's father called out, "Flurry! Hurry up! We're going to visit Chris Kringle today."

Flurry shot out of bed as if an electric

current coursed through his body. Flurry's newfound excitement could not be contained. The boy was in such a hurry that he nearly fell down multiple times before he even got out of his bedroom. It was as if Flurry's short legs could not move him fast enough.

Flurry darted down the stairs, blew past his parents, and was already at the door before he was halted in his tracks. "Whoa! Hold on there, little fella!" exclaimed Flurry's father. "Where's the fire?"

"Indeed! You haven't even had breakfast. Not to mention that you didn't give your mother a hug," Flurry's mom interjected.

"Awww, but Mama, I want to see Santa!" Flurry whined.

Flurry's papa sternly looked at his son. "Now, you know he doesn't like to be called

'Santa'! We've been over this before. His proper name is Christopher, but you are to refer to him as Mr. Kringle."

"Oh yeah! I forgot. Sorry!"

Flurry waited. His mother prepared their meal – though his version of waiting did not resemble patience by any stretch of the imagination. The boy paced to and fro, tapped his feet, and frequently glanced at the door.

Mrs. Snow smiled and shook her head. She understood her boy's impatience, but she also knew full well that Flurry liked to be overly dramatic. "Okay, breakfast is ready," she announced and filled each of their plates. The trio sat at the decorative wood table and ate their breakfast together.

Flurry scarfed down the food in haste. To the untrained eye, it would have appeared to vanish. Flurry loved food very much, but his motivation was not about anything other than his desire to see Christopher Kringle.

Mr. Kringle was quite good with the cubs, and Flurry always loved to see him. Flurry had no idea why they were about to make a trip out to Mr. Kringle's house so early in the morning, but none of that mattered. All that mattered was that he would get to see "Santa."

After Flurry's parents finished up their meal, Flurry sighed with relief and hopped down from his chair. In Flurry's mind, his parents moved in slow motion. Mrs. Snow bent down and hugged and kissed her boy on the cheek. She felt so loved when she got another round of hugs and kisses from her beloved husband, too. As her cuties departed she called out, "Have a good day, my boys!

Flurry, please behave. I love you!"

"I will, Mama!" Flurry assured his mother. "I love you, too! Okay, goodbye!"

Mr. Snow waved goodbye and closed the front door. His wife watched from the window with a smile. She observed Flurry's exuberant behavior. The cub pulled on his father's arm in an attempt to make him walk faster. Flurry was a very excitable young cub, and his presence always livened the mood anywhere he went. Mrs. Snow was so proud of her son and was optimistic about his meeting with Christopher.

The path to the Kringle house was very beautiful that morning. The fresh snow sparkled like glitter in the moon's rays. The light cast long shadows from the evergreen trees and out across the curves of the landscape. The birds chirped, and the absence of wind made the morning feel ever more serene. The stillness of the air amplified the sound of their footsteps. This dynamic made their stride seem like stomping.

After only a brief stretch along the path, Flurry stopped dead in his tracks. "What's the matter, son?" his father asked.

The cub spun around and ran back toward the house. Being quick on his feet, Mr. Snow snagged Flurry by the scarf. Mr. Snow found himself amused as Flurry ran in place. "Slow down there, my boy! What has you troubled?" he asked.

"I forgot to draw a picture for Santa. I don't want to go without drawing him a picture!" Flurry answered. He attempted to escape his father's strong grip, but to no avail.

"Chris will understand. It'll be okay. How about this? Next time you can make two drawings for him. Okay?" Mr. Snow reasoned with his son and won.

"Okay!" Flurry answered. He quickly spun back around, and took off toward the Kringle house again.

"What has gotten into you?" Mr. Snow asked.

"Well, now we have to make up for lost time. Hurry, Papa!" Flurry shouted back at his father, who now trailed behind.

Mr. Snow smiled with admiration. "Slow down!" he shouted to his son, who was quickly about to vanish around the tree up ahead of them. He picked up his pace in an attempt to catch up with his boy.

For Flurry, the walk to Mr. Kringle's home got more exciting with each step.

Flurry imagined what they would say to each other, and whether or not Mr. Kringle would have any goodies. Flurry loved all manner of sweets, especially anything made of chocolate. Flurry's mouth watered as he thought of hot chocolate and fresh, moist chocolate chip cookies.

Before long, they arrived at Mr. Kringle's house, and it was quite a sight to see. The home was very large with many rooms. To Flurry, it was like a castle. Flurry had dreamed of exploring the magnificent structure. The possibilities of adventure in such a place seemed endless. *Oh, if only Sunny and Bliz could see this*, Flurry thought to himself. Bliz was another of Flurry's close friends, as well as his cousin.

When Flurry approached the door, his size really came into perspective. Granted,

Flurry was just a teddy bear cub, small enough for a child to carry, but Mr. Kringle stood more than six feet tall. So when Flurry gazed up at the door, it seemed as if a giant might live in the house.

"Are you going to knock?" asked Flurry's father.

Flurry was nervous. He was not sure why, but he was. He inched forward, closed his eyes, raised his right paw, and made a knocking motion. However, he did not feel his paw connect with the door, nor did he hear a knocking sound. He opened his eyes and peered up to find Mr. Kringle instead of the door. The lofty man had already opened it to greet his visitors.

"Well hello there, little fellow." Mr. Kringle spoke to Flurry in a warm and inviting voice. "What brings you here so early in the morning?"

Flurry's shyness faded away at the sound of Kringle's voice. The cub was now excited to see the man who towered above him. Flurry ran forward and hugged his leg. Mr. Kringle bent down, scooped Flurry up, and set him upon his shoulders. "Weeeee!" Flurry cried out and giggled with excitement.

Mr. Kringle outstretched his arm and invited his second guest in. "Welcome! Welcome! Please, come in."

Mr. Snow shook off the loose snow from his feet and entered. When he stepped inside, Mr. Snow's eyes opened wide to take in the view. The house had many rooms. At least one fireplace, many comfortable-looking pieces of furniture, and a large collection of tapestries could be seen throughout the place. After he closed the door behind them, Mr. Kringle inquired, "May I interest you in something to drink?" He looked up at the cub on his shoulders and continued. "Perhaps some hot chocolate for you?"

Before Mr. Snow could answer, Flurry chimed in. "I want some!"

"No, thank you. I'm fine," answered Mr. Snow. They entered a large room, and Flurry's father took the seat nearest to the fireplace.

"Sweetheart, would you be so kind as to bring out some hot chocolate and fresh cookies for our welcome guests?" Mr. Kringle asked his wife. Her name was Catherine and she had long, red hair, a slender face, and green eyes. She was very beautiful to behold.

"Why, certainly! Flurry, would you like to have some marshmallows in your hot chocolate?" Catherine asked.

"Sure! Yum, yum!" Flurry enthusiastically replied.

Christopher chuckled. Flurry was a source of great amusement and adoration. Mr. Kringle placed Flurry on the couch, and sat down in his high-backed seat. Mr. Snow rested in the other armchair at the opposite end of the coffee table. Flurry had the whole couch to himself. The fireplace crackled from across from the coffee table. Warm flames reflected in the cub's eyes.

Flurry was enamored with Mr. Kringle's appearance. Christopher wore a long, crimson-colored coat that extended to the middle of his thighs. It was adorned with gold trim and decorative needlework along the hem. Christopher's coat was the most eye-catching part of his attire. He also wore a sky blue shirt, a forest green scarf, black pants, and dark brown boots made out of fine leather.

It was at this time that Catherine brought out the treats. Flurry guzzled the hot chocolate down in a rush. Mr. Kringle chortled, "Slow down there, lad. There's plenty! No need to rush."

Flurry pulled the steaming mug away from his face which revealed a hot chocolate mustache formed on his upper lip. Both, the Kringles and the cub's father laughed. "I can see that he's just as adorable as ever," Catherine mentioned.

"Well, we have his mother to thank for that," Mr. Snow answered.

Christopher turned to Mr. Snow and

cleared his throat. A more solemn tone came to his voice. "Well then, let's get down to business, shall we? I hear you've been having some trouble with this little one."

Flurry had been in the process of eating a cookie when he suddenly froze in place, his mouth wide open. In Flurry's shock, he dropped the cookie from his paw. He had been tricked, or so Flurry thought. "Wait a minute! What do you mean? What does he mean, Papa?" Flurry looked back and forth between the two males. The cub was in disbelief.

Mr. Kringle interjected, "Don't worry, dear Flurry, we're here to help you, not to punish you."

Flurry could not believe his ears. He thought they were going to have a day of fun, not a day of being lectured. Flurry lost his appetite and put the cookie, which he had picked back up, on the plate.

Mr. Snow began the conversation. "Thank you for meeting with us under such short notice. I didn't know what else to do, so my wife and I agreed that you might have a solution to our dilemma."

"Well, I can't make any promises, but I'll do my best to give you sound advice," Mr. Kringle answered. The man grabbed his chin, leaned forward, and gave his full attention to Mr. Snow.

Flurry's father continued. "You see, Flurry has a big heart, and he means well, but he just keeps getting himself into trouble." Mr. Snow went on for quite a while. He recited numerous examples which also included Flurry's more recent blunders with tree climbing, breaking the vase, and toppling the pile of honey jars at the grocery store.

After Mr. Snow had exhausted all of his examples, Mr. Kringle turned to Flurry and gazed upon him with his deep, brown eyes. Flurry looked up, and their eyes met. Flurry could see the empathy in Christopher's countenance.

Mr. Kringle stroked his dark but graying beard and spoke up, "Flurry, come here, little fellow. Sit on my lap." Mr. Kringle patted his lap twice to indicate where he wanted Flurry to sit.

Flurry climbed down from the couch and scurried to Christopher. The cub reached up at the man. Mr. Kringle bent over, picked Flurry up, and set him on his lap. "Let's hear your version of this story, shall we?"

Flurry's mouth moved a mile a minute as

he detailed every event that took place and how he had gotten into so many messes. By the time Flurry made it through all of his stories, he was in tears.

"I didn't mean to get into trouble. I just wanted to play and have fun." Flurry struggled to get the words out between sobs.

Tears had formed in Christopher and Mr. Snow's eyes as they each gave Flurry their undivided attention. Christopher reached over, wiped Flurry's tears away, and looked upon the little bear with pity.

After a brief moment of introspection, Christopher asked, "Flurry, I tell you what. How about I give you a job?"

"A job? Wow! What kind of job?" Flurry was so excited by the idea. It was as if he had not even cried moments ago – it was uncanny how the cub's emotions could change so quickly, as if the previous emotional state had not even happened.

Mr. Snow was dumbfounded by what Mr. Kringle had to say. After all of the time they spent with him, it did not seem logical that Christopher's conclusion was to give Flurry a job.

Mr. Kringle continued. "Well, as I see it, I think that giving you some responsibilities might be of help. I believe that if you put your talents to good use, you can benefit from this greatly. Having some duties will occupy your time and help you to set priorities. I can clearly see that you're talented, creative, and have a big heart. You like to bring joy into the lives of others. So why not put you in charge of my teddy bear production line at the toy factory? There you can have influence, and have a say in what the bears look like before we manufacture and ship them to the toy stores. What do you say to that?"

Flurry's jaw practically hit the floor. "Wow! That would be great!"

"Okay, then! You start first thing tomorrow morning. I expect you to be at the factory, bright and early. Be on time! One of the workers, named Jinja, will greet you at the door and give you a tour of the facility. If you have any questions, Jinja can answer them for you."

Christopher stood up, carried Flurry to the front door, and set him down at the threshold. Mr. Snow shook Christopher's hand and said, "Thank you so much for listening to us. I hope your idea will work. Thank you, again, for such a great opportunity!"

Christopher smiled and replied, "You're more than welcome, Mr. Snow. If you ever need anything, don't hesitate to ask …"

Before Christopher could finish his thought, Flurry quickly cut in with, "Oh! In that case, may I have another cookie?"

"Flurry! I taught you better than that!" Mr. Snow reprimanded his son. "Besides, I don't think that's what he meant."

Christopher erupted in laughter. Mr. Snow and Flurry did not expect that reaction. "Of course you can! Take the rest of them. I'm not expecting any visitors for a while, and I'm trying to watch my waistline, if you know what I mean. If you don't take them, I might eat them all myself."

Catherine brought out a little bag filled with the remaining cookies. "What do you say?" Mr. Snow asked his son.

"Thank you, Santa!" Flurry answered.

Christopher paused for a moment with a perplexed expression on his face. "You know my name is Christopher, right? If you keep calling me 'Santa', it's going to catch on, and then everyone will be calling me that."

"Oh, sorry! I forgot," Flurry apologized.

"It's all right. I'm pleased to see your countenance improve. Enjoy your day, and Jinja will see you at the factory tomorrow morning."

"Okay, goodbye!" Flurry exclaimed with much vigor. They waved farewell to one another. Flurry looked over his shoulder until Christopher finally closed the door behind him. Flurry was gleeful, and his joy was so radiant that you would almost swear he glowed like the sun. At this time of year, the sun had not been seen in a long time. However, this day, Flurry made up for it.

Flurry munched on his cookies as he and his papa trekked back home. With chocolate all around his mouth and crumbs upon his scarf, Flurry fantasized about what it would be like at the toy factory. At that moment, nothing else in the world mattered. Flurry was at peace. He ate from his bag full of cookies and marched along, happy and content.

CHAPTER 4
THE TOY FACTORY

The next day could not come soon enough. Flurry barely got an ounce of sleep. He spent his night deep in thought. His imagination ran wild with ideas of what the next day would bring. He envisioned what he would make the plush bears look like, what he would call them, and how he would spend his entire day playing with them.

At the cusp of another day of darkness, Flurry sat up wide-eyed and bushy-tailed – or at least he would have been if he had a tail. He was raring to go and was on his feet before his parents had even opened their eyes. However, Flurry had a way of making sure you were up when he needed you to be.

Flurry ran to his parents' bedroom door and pushed it open. The door creaked to let in a beam of orange light. The radiant source cast Flurry's long, dark shadow along the floorboards and up onto the bed of two plush bears that slept soundly.

Flurry was perplexed by this. *That's strange*, Flurry thought to himself. It was odd that they were not up yet, especially since they both knew it was his big day. *Why wouldn't they be awake to send me on my way?* Flurry pondered.

Well, that did not stop him from making sure that they woke up. Flurry panted and climbed up onto the bed. He rushed over and gently nudged his mother's shoulder. "Mama! Mama! Time to get up!" Unfortunately for the cub, there was no response. Flurry turned to his father and tugged on his ear. "Papa! Papa! I have to go to work!" His parents snored all the more. When Flurry deduced that it would be the only reply he got, he took it to the next level.

Not to go unnoticed, Flurry jumped up and down, and he shouted, "Wake up! Wake up! Wake up!"

"Ahhh!" screamed the Snow couple as they shot up from their pillows. They were so startled that they nearly fell out of the bed.

Flurry's parents were considerably flustered, and understandably so. Nobody would like to be rallied from sleep in that manner. "Flurry! Do you know what time it is? Why did you wake us up so early?" Flurry's father shouted.

"I have to go to work now! I just thought I'd let you know. Okay, goodbye!" Flurry quickly informed the couple and then promptly hopped down from the bed.

"Sweetie, you don't have to go to work for another three hours. Go back to bed," the boy's mother pleaded with her son and yawned.

Flurry was surprised. His excitement and impatience blinded him to this fact. "Awww!" moped the cub as he slowly shuffled back out of the room and left his parents' door open behind him.

With a sigh, Mrs. Snow got out of bed. She looked back at her husband, who was also about to get out of bed. "No. Just stay there. You need your rest. I'll go check on

Flurry." Mrs. Snow gently pushed her husband back down in the bed, and pulled the blanket up over him. She kissed him on the cheek, and he was fast asleep by the time she reached the door.

Mrs. Snow approached Flurry's room and peeked in. He impatiently paced back and forth beside his bed. "Sweetie, I understand that you're excited, but you can't rush things. Your time will come soon enough."

"I wish I could! I wish the sun was up! That would get everyone out of bed!" Flurry exclaimed.

Suddenly, without any explanation, the sky changed color. Light now peeked from the horizon. In a matter of minutes, the sun had risen into the sky. "That's strange!" exclaimed Mrs. Snow. "Flurry, do you see that?"

Flurry ran up to the window and looked out. "Wow! It's the sun! Time to go!" Flurry's excitement was instantly rekindled. The cub did not even bat an eye at the strange event which took place right outside his window.

The land of Mezarim was a place filled with wonder. However, it was in the middle of winter, and the sun was not expected to be seen for a few more months. Mrs. Snow was perplexed by the sudden sunrise. In all her life, she had never seen something that strange.

Flurry ran back to his father's bedroom to wake him up again. "Papa! Papa! It's time to get up!"

"Flurry, you were just in here only a few minutes ago," Flurry's father grunted. You could hear a bit of a growl in his frustrated tone.

Mrs. Snow walked in after Flurry and grabbed her boy by the shoulders to back him away from the bed. "Calm down, Flurry," she insisted.

"Okay, Mama. Sorry," her son replied. The cub stood there quietly, with his arms behind his back. He looked absolutely adorable.

"Flurry's right, it's time to get up. I have no explanation for it. The sun just suddenly did in minutes what should've taken it months to do," Mrs. Snow relayed to her husband. Her voice revealed her insecurity, related to the strange turn of events.

"That's odd," her husband replied. He sat up and rubbed his eyes. He then got out of bed, walked over to the window, and looked out. Sure enough, the sun was just above the horizon. "That's the strangest thing I've ever seen. I'll have to ask Chris what he makes of this." Flurry's parents exchanged concerned glances with each other before Mr. Snow shrugged his shoulders and put on his bow tie.

"Papa, come on! I'm going to be late!" Flurry's voice was riddled with deep concern. The cub did not want to mess up his first day on the job. He wanted to make Mr. Kringle and his parents equally proud of him.

All three of the bears went downstairs. Mrs. Snow fixed Flurry breakfast and made sack lunches for both her son and her husband. Before he left, Flurry gave his mother a hug, then out the door he went.

Flurry and his father had not gone far before Mrs. Snow came out of the house.

She stood at the threshold of the door, and waved to them as they strode down the cobblestone path.

"Have a good day, my sweethearts!" she called out to them.

"Thank you! We will!" they both hollered back to her in unison. Flurry walked backwards so he could wave at his mother.

"Okay, goodbye!" Flurry shouted. The cub perceived that she looked proud of him. It warmed Flurry's heart and made him even more dedicated to doing his best at the toy factory.

Mr. Snow and his son traversed the winding path up and down gradual slopes of the landscape. The walk to the factory was a long one but certainly very scenic. The workings of a beautiful day were at hand, but that morning things were not as they should be. The village was in chaos. The bears ran all around to get ready for the day. It was as if everyone had overslept and was now frantic to make it to their destinations on time. Mr. Snow had never seen anything like it before.

Uncertain of what else to do, they continued down the hill into a valley, where the factory was positioned next to a meandering river. The factory was small and was the only landmark to be found in the valley on that side of the bank. A thick forest sat at the opposite riverbank. On a normal day, Flurry would have seen the forest as a place to be explored, and the promise of adventure would have beckoned to him, but not this day. Today, Flurry's mind was set on the impact he could make on the plush bear production line.

As they approached the factory, they could see many bears rush to get inside. Christopher Kringle stood outside the front doors and greeted them as they entered.

Christopher was a welcomed sight. He brought comfort to everyone when they saw that he had a smile on his face, spoke calmly, and frequently chuckled. "No worries, my friends, everything is fine. We're just off to a late start today, nothing to get too flustered about."

As Mr. Snow and Flurry drew near, Christopher looked at Flurry and smiled. The man had a twinkle in his eye. Flurry was uncertain what it meant, but Christopher had something on his mind. "Well, hello there! I'm proud to see the two of you here this fine morning." After Christopher greeted them, he turned his attention more directly at Flurry. He squatted down to be closer to the cub's eye level. "It does my heart joy to see you here, my little friend. Are you excited about your first day?"

"Uh huh!" Flurry exclaimed and nodded his head vigorously.

"Good!" Christopher patted the bear on the head, chuckled, and continued. "Well, I should be headed back home. Jinja will be here shortly. As you can see, this day has started off rather unconventionally." Christopher winked at Flurry and then tipped his cap to Mr. Snow. "Good day to you, Mr. Snow."

"Good day to you, too," he answered back. Flurry's father then added, "Wait! Do you know what's going on? Why is the sun up?"

Christopher laughed a loud and boisterous

laugh before he replied, "I have a hunch!" He directed his gaze upon Flurry and said, "Flurry, be sure to have fun, and be good!" Christopher turned away and continued his trek up the icy path.

"I will! Okay, goodbye!" Flurry fervently waved.

"Flurry, I have to go in and work now. Just wait here and Jinja will be out to greet you soon." Flurry's father gave his cub a warm hug and said, "I'm proud of you, son. Have a good day at work. I love you!"

"Thank you, Papa! I love you, too!" Flurry replied to his father. Mr. Snow vanished behind the factory doors.

Flurry did not have long to wait before the doors reopened. A bear with red fur, glasses, and a mug of hot tea came out to greet him. "Hello! I'm Jinja. I presume that you must be Flurry."

"Yes, I am," Flurry replied. The cub was fixated on the yellow sickle shape on Jinja's chest. Jinja looked a bit unique from other teddy bears that Flurry had seen. The individual that created Jinja wanted him to resemble a moon bear. Flurry knew this because moon bears have a crescent moon shape on their chests.

Jinja was one of Mr. Kringle's most trusted workers. He was hardworking, dedicated, and easygoing. He primarily did most of his work with clay and pottery. He also had a reputation for always having his mug of tea close at hand.

"Please, come in! You must be cold standing out here," Jinja insisted.

"Nah, the cold never bothers me. I'm fine!" Flurry assured him.

Flurry entered, and Jinja closed the doors behind them. It was nice and warm inside, and Flurry felt even more ardent than before – if that was possible. He could hear other bears hum, whistle, and sing while they built a variety of different toys and dolls. Many of the toys were to be given away to all of the children in the region every Christmas. Yet, some of the toys were also sent to stores in another world named Earth. Flurry's world and Earth were connected through an invisible gateway at each world's northern pole. The money from the toys helped Christopher purchase materials that he and the teddy bears would need on a day-to-day basis or for food and supplies that were given to anyone in need.

Unlike the legends, Christopher could not possibly make it to each and every house in one night. It took multiple trips to and from Ursus. He made his rounds throughout the night and well into the day at the northernmost city in Mezarim named Polaris. Though Flurry's village was considered to be part of the North Pole, it was not truly the northernmost point on the map. However, it was far enough north that most people would not squabble over such details.

Before Flurry had much of a chance to take everything in, another bear came and greeted him. This bear was very large and round. He looked a lot like a panda bear, but instead of being black and white, this bear was purple and white. He wore a tool belt, similar to what Flurry's father wore, but this belt held mechanic tools instead of carpentry tools.

"Flurry, I'd like you to meet my good friend Mojo. He's responsible for repairing everything here at the …" Jinja did not get to finish what he was about to say before Mojo interrupted him.

"Not everything!" the panda interjected.

"Well, everything mechanical," Jinja quickly corrected himself.

"Well, technically, I just repair the equipment."

"Why do you always have to correct me?" Jinja shot back.

"I don't always correct you."

"Yes, you do!"

Mojo put his paws on his hips and added, "I only correct you when you're wrong."

"You correct me all the time," Jinja insisted. He now looked quite flustered.

"Then I guess you're wrong a lot," Mojo

returned in a smug tone. A smirk was present upon his face.

"Oh no you didn't! How could you say that?" Jinja's shock and disbelief were clear. If his fur was not already red, it would have been easier to see how flushed his face had become.

"I just did!"

"It's always the same with you! You always start arguments with me!"

"I'm not arguing!"

"Yes, you are!"

"No, I'm not!"

In the midst of their debate, Flurry felt that it was not anywhere close to being over. The cub slipped past them. Flurry decided it was best to just give himself the tour.

Flurry went from room to room and observed all of the grand craftsmanship that went into each and every toy. The other bears were fine artisans. Flurry marveled at all of the wonderful toys that he desperately desired to play with.

Flurry had already toured the entire plant and was at the boxing and shipping end of the factory when Jinja finally caught back up with him.

Jinja jogged up to Flurry. "There you are!" Jinja exclaimed, out of breath. "I've been looking all over for you. Where have you been?" He stood next to Flurry and panted.

"Well, I didn't want to interrupt your argument, so I showed myself around," Flurry answered.

"Oh! That! Well, he always does that. It's not a big deal." Jinja shrugged off the incident as if it were not worth mentioning.

He took a sip of his tea, pushed his glasses back up, and pointed to the shipping line. "Well, as you can see, this is where we box and ship all of our toys out. Someday you'll get to see your very own toy designs be shipped from here."

Flurry already envisioned it, while he observed the boxes get dragged along the conveyor belt in front of him.

Jinja continued. "But remember. Safety first! You don't want to get too close to the conveyor belt. If you were to fall onto the belt, you might get boxed up and shipped off. That would be very bad!"

Flurry immediately stepped away from the railing. The cub now felt fearful to go anywhere near the conveyor belt. As Jinja continued the last leg of the tour, Flurry quickly followed after him. He did not want to be left alone anywhere near the conveyor belt.

Flurry's first day on the job was a blast, and everything went smoothly. He enjoyed meeting the other bears and being shown around the factory.

Flurry quickly filled his role as the lead input advisor on the teddy bear assembly line. Flurry presented many ideas and put forth every ounce of creativity into the creation of the various teddy bears and other plush dolls. The adults loved his input, for he had ideas that only a cub could think of. Christopher Kringle was wise to have Flurry there – after all, if you wanted to make something a child would like, who better to ask than a child?

A great deal of time passed. Whether it was days, weeks, months, or years was irrelevant. Flurry had earned his keep and was a vital part of the process. It was as the saying goes, "Time flies when you're having fun", and Flurry certainly had fun. He especially liked quality control. That was just a fancy way of saying: "Play with the toys."

Flurry did his job well, and things were about to become even better after his epiphany.

One night, while Flurry lay in bed, he had a brilliant idea. He pondered why he had not thought of such a brilliant product sooner. He thought to himself, *If I'm the cutest teddy bear ever, and everyone loves me, then why not make teddy bears that look like me? They'll be the most popular item ever!*

Now, we all have character flaws, and Flurry had some of his own. His biggest flaw was that he was overly vain about his physical appearance. Many had praised him for his cute looks. The compliments happened so frequently that it had gone to Flurry's head. The cub was in desperate need of some humility, and would eventually get some in a most unexpected way.

Flurry had been quick to implement his new teddy bear line. He named them Flakey bears. The Flakey bears looked exactly like Flurry, and he was supremely confident that they would become Mr. Kringle's hottest-selling item.

One night, a few days before an upcoming holiday, Flurry was about to lock up at the factory. As he turned the key he thought about the Flakey bear line. He was so proud of what he had achieved that he decided to go back inside and take another look at them before he ventured home.

Flurry walked back inside and skipped through factory. He occasionally stopped to look at a toy from time-to-time. He then went into the shipping area where the Flakey bears got boxed up and shipped out to toy stores. The factory was quite busy. It prepared numerous boxes for the holiday season.

Flurry felt so proud of himself. He had done a good job, stayed out of trouble, made his parents proud, lived up to Mr. Kringle's expectations, and made the cutest teddy bears ever – other than himself, of course. He was the best, and he knew it – or so he thought.

Flurry imagined being famous, and thought about how everyone would someday carry their very own Flakey bears around with them. His head was up in the clouds so high that he forgot Jinja's warning about the conveyor belt. Normally Flurry would never go near it, but he had a momentary lapse in judgment during this time of self-adoration.

Flurry could hear the automated boxing that took place. Giant mechanical arms repeated their automated motion. The large metal hand picked up and placed one Flakey after another into large boxes and sealed them up. More bears glided down a slide and onto the conveyor belt, ready to be boxed.

It was difficult for Flurry to see over the guard rail. The little cub climbed up each rung of the barrier between himself and the conveyor belt below. He peered over to watch the process that took place.

Flurry admired his creation and lingered in further thoughts about how cute he and the Flakey bears were. Before Flurry realized what had happened, he lost his balance and fell onto the conveyor belt.

Flurry panicked and attempted to get down from it, but a large metal hand snatched Flurry up, and placed him in a box with the other Flakey bears.

Flurry screamed and shouted for help, but nobody could hear him. Everyone had left for the night, and the toy factory had a policy that nobody was ever to be alone near the running equipment. Flurry broke that rule and was now in a lot of trouble.

Flurry toiled to climb up out of the box, but every time he made some progress, another Flakey bear got dropped into the box right on top of him. This knocked the cub down repeatedly.

Flurry continued to struggle and climb. A glimmer of hope worked its way into Flurry's thoughts when he neared the top of the box without any more Flakey bears being added to the collection. However, his hope was quickly doused when the parcel moved, and the flaps were folded down over the opening.

It was suddenly dark, and the only thing Flurry could see was a thin line of light, where the flaps met. That tiny bit of light was quickly extinguished when the sound of packaging tape was heard. Tape stretched across the surface of the box. Flurry had just been sealed in, and the box was labeled to be shipped to a far off country named Middleasia.

CHAPTER 5
TOY STORE CHASE

Darkness and despair overtook Flurry while he lay among the Flakey bears. There was not a shred of hope that he could get out. Flurry regretted his actions, and wished he had not gone back into the factory to marvel at himself. Flurry did not know how long he had lain among the Flakey bears. The pitch black darkness snuffed out any means to distinguish the amount of time which had passed. Middleasia resided on Earth and was exceptionally far from Ursus. Flurry deduced that days might have passed since the cub had been in transit.

He felt hungry, but that was purely in his mind, because he had no need for food – eating was simply a recreational pleasure to him. Flurry loved the savor of delicious food, and now missed it more than ever. He especially loved sweets. Flurry visualized the delectable tastes of freshly baked sugar cookies, the peppermint flavor of candy canes, and the creamy goodness of hot chocolate. It was an unbearable torment.

Flurry continued to lie among the soft fur of the lifeless Flakey bears. He thought about his parents and how much he missed them. As he reminisced about being home with his mother and father, the cub cried. Tears streamed down his face. Remorse and regret overwhelmed him. Flurry wanted to go back home, but he was trapped.

In Ursus, things were not much better. Mr. and Mrs. Snow quickly noticed the absence of their deeply beloved son. It was not like Flurry to not be home on time. Their worry quickly turned into action. They went to the factory and searched for him, but found it closed up and the lights out. Christopher Kringle joined the search. He and a team of bears combed the factory. They were too late. The boxes had already been shipped out, and not a single one of them would have ever guessed to look for Flurry there.

They searched the factory from top to bottom, but turned up nothing – not even a clue. Nobody had any idea what to do next. They were about to abandon their search within the factory, and move on to another area until Jinja noticed something odd. The automated process for packaging the Flakey bears had not ever been known to make a mistake. The machines kept an accurate count of how many bears were packed into the boxes. Each box would be filled with twenty Flakey bears before being shipped out. However, one Flakey bear had been left behind. Jinja and Mojo stood over the lone plush bear that remained. They gazed upon the single bear that lay on the conveyor belt, and contemplated the meaning of its presence. It perplexed them, to say the least, for there should not have been any Flakey bears left over.

Jinja quickly brought this newfound clue to the attention of Mr. Kringle, and the rest of the search team. "Oh my!" Flurry's mother gasped. "You don't suppose Flurry was in one of the boxes that got shipped off, do you?" She struggled to fight back her tears, but was unable to hold them at bay for very long. Mr. Snow quickly threw his arm around his wife as she sobbed. However, he too fought back his own tears.

Christopher felt deep empathy for them both, and tried to comfort Mrs. Snow. "There's no need to worry, my dear. If Flurry has been shipped out with the Flakey bears, he will turn up at one of the toy stores. From there, we can retrieve him. He'll be fine." He meant well, but his words were not enough to stop the steady stream that freely flowed from her eyes.

"There's nothing we can do until the packages reach their destinations. Then we'll know where Flurry has arrived, and we can act accordingly. For now, we can keep

Flurry in our thoughts." Christopher concluded their meeting, escorted the bears out the front doors, and locked up.

It is uncertain how long Flurry or his parents cried. They thought about, and missed, each other tremendously. However, Flurry's tears were abruptly halted when he felt a sharp jolt. The box suddenly stopped moving, and he could hear the faint sound of voices. He could not recognize the muffled dialogue through the box and all of the Flakey bears piled on top of and around him.

Flurry felt relieved and thought to himself, *It must be one of the other workers. They found me! I'm saved!*

Flurry's excitement continued to grow as different sounds permeated the box where he waited. He heard the sounds of cutting and the removal of packaging tape. A sliver of light beamed into the box. Then, in an instance, light flooded into the box. With the flaps now drawn back Flurry jumped up from among the plush bears. Impassioned, he exclaimed, "Here I am! Yay! I'm saved!"

Flurry was more surprised than the men that stood by the box. He was not in the toy factory in Ursus. In fact, he was not even on his own world. The individuals that stood in Flurry's immediate vicinity were not teddy bears, nor Mr. Kringle. Flurry glanced about in disbelief at the three men. They each wore matching red shirts that read: "Middleasia's Toy Emporium."

Flurry realized he was on Earth, and that people from this world were not accustomed to a living, breathing teddy bear who could speak. Flurry instantly fell back into the box and laid as still as he possibly could. He kept silent to blend in with the Flakey bears. Flurry wondered, *Did they notice me? I hope they didn't notice.* However, it was difficult to not notice a teddy bear jump up from a box and begin to speak.

The shock and awe of having seen a living teddy bear was almost palpable. You could have heard a pin drop in the still silence of the room. The toy store workers contemplated if the bear simply had a voice box installed or if it was really alive. After all, if it was genuinely real they could make a fortune off of him. In fact, this could be their lucky break. Such a find was unprecedented.

When each employee realized the amount of money that they could make from this discovery, the workers all rushed to the box. They pushed and shoved each other away.

Each man competitively scrambled to find which bear was Flurry.

Luckily for Flurry, he was very clever. He quickly burrowed deep into the box which made it very difficult for the toy store workers to find him. One of them grabbed the box, flipped it over, and dumped all of the bears out onto the floor. He frantically checked each of them one-by-one.

"Guard the door! Make sure it can't escape," one of the workers shouted. Another of the men quickly jogged over to the door and stood by.

As careful as the men were to take precautions, Flurry had already made his escape plan. He realized that the door handle was too high for him to reach, but he waited patiently for his opportunity. While they combed through the box's contents, it was only a matter of time before they found him.

Before long, Flurry's moment arrived. It was as if fate had been on his side. Someone opened the door from the other side and entered the unpacking area. It was an important-looking female in a gray suit. She strode in with purpose and authority. When she gazed upon the mess, she gasped. "What in the world are you doing? Why would you dump all of our merchandise on the floor like that? Are you insane? Pick those bears up right now and either put them back in that box or out on the shelves before I decide to fire all three of you!"

The men stumbled over themselves and attempted to give the lady an answer, but they melted before her authoritative demeanor. They picked up the Flakey bears, brushed them off, and placed them back into the box. She turned around to head back out into the store. Flurry made a run for the door. The men bellowed out, "Get that bear!" but it was too late. Flurry had slipped through the door and into the toy store.

The boss heard their shout and turned back. "What was that?" Her employees shrugged and returned to their work until she walked back out.

The workers each stood there for a moment, uncertain about what they should do. They knew if they did not pick up the Flakey bears they would be in trouble, but if they could catch Flurry they would be rich. It did not take them long to weigh their options. The three men concluded to continue their hunt to find and capture Flurry. They ran for the door in hot pursuit.

Flurry dashed down the aisles of the toy

store while he looked for a safe haven. He ran as fast as his little legs would take him.

As careful as Flurry tried to be to avoid being detected, a little girl caught sight of him. Her mouth dropped open with awe. She vigorously pulled at her mother's arm, and called out to her in earnest, "Mommy! Mommy! Look! Look! That teddy bear is real!"

The little girl's mother looked around, but saw nothing. She peered down at her daughter and answered, "Yes, that's nice, dear," then resumed her gaze at the shelved products.

Luckily for Flurry, nobody else spotted him. This was in part due to his small stature, the fact that he was light-footed, and that fate had other plans for him. He was very swift on his feet and even swifter with his wit, which enabled him to continue to evade his pursuers.

While Flurry thought about what he should do, he noticed the teddy bear aisle. His face lit up. Flurry whispered to himself, "I know! I'll hide there, but I'll need a disguise."

The cub darted off to an adjacent aisle in search for scissors and glue. He grabbed the needed tools and ran back to the teddy bear aisle. Not an ounce of time was wasted. He hastily cut the tags off one of the plush bears and glued them to himself.

Now disguised, Flurry hid among the other teddy bears on the rack. Normally, he might have stood out a bit, but luckily for Flurry the store already had some of his Flakey bears stocked on the shelves.

Flurry held as still as he possibly could.

He made sure not to even blink. The men worked their way down the aisle. They searched for him high and low.

The self-appointed leader of the three workers ordered one of the others, "Check each and every teddy bear on these shelves!" He then addressed the third member of their team. "We're going to go check the other aisles together." The two men scurried off and left just one man behind to search through the shelved bears.

The employee that remained was in a rush, and wanted to be the first to find Flurry. He did not care enough to put any of the bears back on the shelf after he examined them. The man pulled one off of the shelf, checked it, and then tossed it over his shoulder and onto the floor.

He quickly amassed a pile of plush bears

on the tiled floor. This worked in Flurry's favor. A security guard came down the aisle and caught the store employee in the act. "Hey! You there! Stop what you're doing and come with me!" said the angry security officer.

"Get lost! Can't you see I'm busy here?" retorted the worker in a defensive tone.

The guard was not amused. He marched over, grabbed the man by the arm, and hauled him down the aisle. There they met up with two more of the store's security, the store manager, and the other two workers which were also in custody.

"I don't know what has gotten into the three of you, but you're all fired! Get out of my store!" the lady barked and pointed toward the main entrance. The security guards escorted the three men out of the toy store and into the parking lot.

Flurry remained still and decided to continue to lay low until nightfall. Flurry thought that if he were to just wait until the store closed, he could slip out and make a phone call to Mr. Kringle. Then Flurry could request a pick up. However, Flurry's plans were thwarted when something even more unexpected happened.

Flurry hid long enough that the employees had brushed off and restocked the teddy bears. They cleaned up the entire mess left by the store's former workers. Flurry thought that he was in the clear until a man came down the aisle with his shopping cart.

The gentleman was very tall and slender. He appeared to be in his thirties. The pale skinned male had short brown hair, brown eyes, and a goatee. He looked particularly happy to be in the teddy bear aisle.

He wheeled the cart up in front of the shelf where Flurry sat. He reached for Flurry, picked him up, and held him up in the air. "Wow! This has got to be the cutest teddy bear I've ever seen!" the man exclaimed.

He examined Flurry from every angle. Flurry pretended to be lifeless and held as still as he possibly could. The man sat Flurry in his cart and headed toward the checkout lane. Flurry had already formulated a new escape plan, but the man turned his attention to Flurry again. "My wife has always wanted a teddy bear to add to her collection. She'll be so happy when she sees how cute this one is!" He petted Flurry's soft, white fur.

A young lady greeted the gentleman at the checkout. He placed the bear in her hands. She gave Flurry a hug and told the man, "This is the cutest teddy bear I've ever seen! Where did you find him?"

"He was among the others in the teddy bear aisle," the man answered.

"I'm going to have to buy one of these for myself," the cashier replied.

"It's a Christmas gift for my wife. She's been looking for just the right bear for a long time now. I think I've finally found the perfect one!" the man explained.

"She's so lucky! Your wife will be so happy when she sees this little guy! I'm assuming it's a boy, with that handsome blue scarf. I'm so jealous! I want one, too!" They both laughed in unison.

When he had finished his transaction, the

man carried Flurry out of the building and across the parking lot. Flurry felt tense. It took every bit of effort to not blink or move. He had already conceived a secondary escape plan, but was thwarted again. The cub was placed in the trunk of the man's car before Flurry even realized what had happened.

Trapped! Flurry could not do anything until the man reopened the trunk. When Flurry realized this, he impatiently laid in the dark. The cub felt frustrated that his plans continued to be foiled time-and-time again. After all, there he was, once more, in the midst of total darkness about to be transported to another unknown destination.

Flurry tried numerous times, but was unable to escape the locked trunk. "Awww! Will this ever end?" Flurry muttered to himself.

Flurry took notice of the car's suspension. It wavered when the gentleman got inside. Flurry heard the roar of the engine and soon realized they were on the move. The trunk was not the most comfortable of accommodations, and Flurry felt every bump and hole in the road.

The gentleman, however, could not have been happier. He had finally found the perfect gift to give to his wife for Christmas. Flurry helplessly lay in the trunk. The man drove down the road toward home – a small town named Haengbokville.

CHAPTER 6
A LESSON TO LEARN

The gentleman arrived at a lovely stone house with a chimney and a big yard. The house was historic and well-maintained. He turned onto the paved driveway that led to the backyard. The pavement wrapped around a maple tree and then back toward the entrance of a garage which connected to the back of the house.

The man parked the car and quickly opened the trunk to get his special gift out for his wife. He entered the house cautiously, to keep his surprise from being discovered. His wife, Lynn, was hard at work. She sat at the dining room table and graded her student's tests. She worked as an instructor at the university in the city of Miso.

The couple was very young. They were clearly married, as their matching wedding rings revealed. Lynn looked to be in her mid-twenties. She was very beautiful with her long, black hair and thin oriental features. She also wore a pair of black-framed glasses, which made her look even more adorable.

It was evident why her husband loved her so much. She had a sweet essence.

Her husband wanted to see her face light up at the sight of his Christmas present, but he restrained himself, went into their bedroom, and hid the little bear under their bedspread. *There! She won't realize that there's something under her blanket until she gets into bed. Then she'll see the surprise I have waiting for her*, he thought to himself before he left the room and closed the door after him.

Finally! Flurry thought internally. The cub peeked out from under the blanket. "I thought he'd never leave," he muttered to himself. "What should I do now? I wonder if … oooh!" Flurry gazed over at the young lady's mobile phone that sat on the nightstand beside him. Flurry's paw shot out from under the covers and snagged the phone more quickly than you could blink. The cub hid under the blanket and dialed.

The phone number that Flurry used was not a typical phone number, since it was a direct line to Christopher Kringle. Flurry thought to himself, *Maybe Santa can swing by and pick me up.*

Flurry's phone call was met with much joy and anticipation. Flurry's mother was the first to talk on the phone with him. They shed tears together and told each other how much they missed and loved one other. Then Flurry spoke with his father and apologized for making them worry, but his father was exceptionally understanding and was relieved to know that his beloved son was safe.

Christopher got on the phone last. Flurry explained his entire story. He went into detail about how all he wanted to do was to look at how cute his Flakey bears were. Flurry went on about how one thing led to another, which stranded him in the home of strangers in a foreign land named Middleasia.

Flurry wanted to be sure that he got every detail in, but this worked against him. After Christopher heard what had caused the incident in the first place, his countenance changed from compassionate to disciplinary.

Christopher cleared his throat. With a stern voice he replied, "Well, young one, that's quite the story. Seeing as how your vanity got you into this mess, I deem it fitting to leave you there until you can learn humility."

There was a long pause with nothing but silence. Flurry could not believe his ears. In fact, Flurry felt outraged that "Santa" would say that. Uncertain of what to say, Flurry could only manage to blurt out, "But!"

Flurry's short and incomplete response

was cut off by Christopher Kringle's continued discourse. "Now, this couple you're staying with, I know of them. The Great King made them known to me a while ago. Now I see why. They've been unable to have any children of their own, though they very much have longed to. I can state with confidence that they'll love and cherish you deeply.

"This disciplinary action is to humble you and teach you to learn that you shouldn't be so stuck on your looks. What's important is what someone's like on the inside, not how they appear on the outside. With time, all beauty fades, but true beauty is that which resides in your deepest parts. True beauty lasts forever. When you can learn humility and prove to me that you've learned to not be so vain, I'll allow you to return."

Mr. Kringle's decree seemed harsh and extreme to Flurry. This would mean that he would not get to play with his buddy Sunny or his cousin Bliz. He would not get to have his mama make hot chocolate for him or get to walk to work with his papa. Flurry could not hold back the flood that burst forth from his eyes. The cub wept bitterly and pleaded with Mr. Kringle. "Please, Santa! I've learned my lesson! Please let me come home!"

"You may come back for short visits, but you cannot truly return until you've learned the value of inner beauty, and shown humility. These are important lessons for raising you up in the ways which are right." Christopher attempted to get Flurry to understand, but the cub could not see the situation outside of his own perspective.

"But, what about Mama and Papa?" he asked. Flurry thought that if he shifted the focus it might convince Christopher of their pain and commute his sentence.

Mr. Kringle saw through Flurry's scheme and reassured him. "I understand what you're saying, and it's true that they'll be sorrowful and miss you. They'll be looked after, and I have something special in mind to ease their pain. They'll also come to visit you from time-to-time, I promise."

Flurry cried all the more. His cries were so loud that there was not any reason why the human couple, which lived in the house, could not or would not hear him – they were in the next room after all.

Christopher continued. "Flurry, please allow me to illustrate my lesson with a personal story. Long ago, I had a little pet named Jack. Jack was a red panda, and he was the cutest of all red pandas. Now, that's saying a lot, since red pandas are inherently adorable. In many ways, his memory reminds me of you. I came across that little fellow during one of my adventures. It was one of the worst winters in decades, and I found him close to death and freezing.

"Well, I couldn't let any poor animal suffer like that; in fact, red pandas are endangered. I took him in and saw to his needs. He looked as if he had been attacked by another animal.

"As time passed, I nursed him back to health. During that time, I had grown quite fond of him. He was like a child to me. In fact, he was my family, before I met Catherine.

"One day, by the blessing of the Great

King, who gave me the ability to work my miracles, I decided to give little Jack the ability to speak, think, and reason, much like you and me.

"It was quite wonderful to be able to teach him new things and to have conversations with him. Over the years we were inseparable. Wherever one was, the other was, too. We were the best of friends. I knew I could rely on him for anything. He assisted me and the other teddy bears in building the first teddy bear village long, long ago. He acted as my emissary to the warrior elves of the south, who are now the protectors of our land. He was instrumental in befriending them. If not for the elves, we wouldn't have our perimeter defense from our enemies and other dangers.

"Yet, despite all of our history together,

Jack had a darker side that lurked deep within his heart. It was like a tiny mustard seed, but time nourished this seed until it grew into something horrible."

"What was that?" Flurry asked him in a deeply concerned voice.

"Well, much like you, everyone adored him. He was loved and praised for his good looks. How could anyone not love him? At least, that's what he thought to himself. This praise and appreciation went to his head. Jack thought of himself as the cutest of all animals. He went so far as to feel that it was the obligation of everyone to compliment him. When someone didn't give him proper acknowledgment, he became angry. He felt that he had been wronged in the worst possible manner.

"His anger grew into bitterness and

resentment. Jack's spiteful feelings and ideas of retaliation upon others blossomed into something more terrifying with each incident that made him feel disrespected.

"Finally, the dark seed in his heart had grown to full maturity. He decided that enough was enough. So Jack set out to exact his revenge. At first, his actions were trivial things, such a pranks and stealing all of the Christmas gifts from the homes of those who hadn't told him that he was cute. However, that was just a taste of something much darker to come.

"Unfortunately, his cruelty didn't stop with such insignificant acts. This red panda's evil heart became so cold that he earned the nickname Frost. With time, he raised up an army to do his bidding. He conquered many kingdoms and demanded that he be praised. At the height of his tyranny, he mandated that he be worshiped as a deity or be put to death.

"His vanity destroyed who he was. I lost my best friend to his own pride. And that was only the beginning of the horrors he brought forth upon our land."

Christopher's voice cracked, but he swallowed hard, took a deep breath, and mustered the strength to finish his thoughts. "Flurry, I'm trying to teach you humility, not to be mean to you. I'm doing this as a means to prevent you from traveling down the path that Jack once took. His heart had grown cold, and his thoughts were like frost. You're a marvelous little bear, and it would break everyone's heart to see you lose your way and your innocence by becoming like Jack. I hope you can understand this."

When Christopher mentioned Flurry's punishment, the cub's frustration returned. Christopher finished the phone conversation with his closing statements. "The people you're with are very loving. You'll be deeply appreciated. As for your mother and father here, I'll inform them of my decision and take special care to ensure that they're comforted. I'll be watching over them and you as well. You may not be aware of my presence, but I'll be keeping an eye on you. So long and farewell, little one. Use this time wisely; it could easily be the best time of your life. My best wishes are with you!"

Flurry felt overwhelmed with disappointment. He had been so sure that "Santa" would bring him back home, but Flurry was wrong. The little cub already missed his parents and friends back in

Ursus.

Flurry pouted. He was now stuck in a foreign land with a couple of strangers. In a moment of rage, Flurry ripped the blanket down from his head to put the phone back on the nightstand. In the middle of his exaggerated display of emotion, Flurry looked up to find the gentleman and his wife at the foot of the bed. The human couple stood with their mouths and eyes wide open in disbelief.

Still in the midst of his tantrum, Flurry glared at them, then threw up his arms, and said, "What? Haven't you seen a talking teddy bear before?" Then, just as quickly as he yanked the blanket down, he jerked it back up over his head, and hid himself from sight.

CHAPTER 7
FLURRY'S NEW LIFE

As time passed, Flurry became like a son to the human couple, and he lovingly called them mommy and daddy to differentiate them from his teddy bear mama and papa. During Flurry's first few weeks in his new home, he explored a lot. He inspected all of the kitchen cabinets, looked under cushions, mattresses, blankets, and inspected the fireplace as well. He quickly took notice of how he would access certain things, especially food items, now that he was in a home where everything was giant compared to him. Nothing was his size or within his reach. It was during all of his exploration that he discovered his mother's collection of plush animals. This was the same collection that Flurry was originally intended to be added to, back when they still believed him to be an ordinary plush bear.

Among the collection were four little plush animals that caught Flurry's attention. The first two looked like lions, though their appearances vastly differed from each other. One was very tall and slender with a long face and a bushy mane. It had a very interesting gaze, as if it were the wisest among the plush animals. It did look like it had been worn out a bit more than the others, possibly from years of use. Strangely, it was without a mouth. Flurry wondered to himself about how that lion could eat, drink, or even talk.

The other lion was very small, with a round face, and a mane that stood up as if it were held in place by static electricity. Flurry wondered if the little one was a scientist, like Albert Einstein, after he noticed how wild and messy that mane was. It was so bushy that Flurry could not see the lion's ears, though they must have been there under all of that fur somewhere.

The next animal in the lineup was a polar bear. This bear had cream-colored fur, black paw pads, and big, black dreamy eyes. It looked like it had been well-loved by its keeper.

Last but not least, Flurry could not help but notice how cute – but grumpy-looking – the little brown bunny was, though he mistakenly thought it was a mouse. As he thought about the bunny, another thought crept into Flurry's mind. *He may be cute, but not as cute as me*. He immediately followed up his thought with *Oops!* when he realized that he had fallen back into the trap of his vanity again.

Due to his curiosity, Flurry attempted to find a way up onto the dresser where the others all sat. Unable to find an easier way up, Flurry climbed. He grunted, huffed, and puffed his way up the dresser until he reached the top. As he stood there, he saw many other plush animals that he had not noticed from his previous vantage point, but he was still interested in the same four that were all lined up in a row next to each other.

"Hello! I'm Flurry!" he called out to them, but they did not reply or even acknowledge his presence at all. Surprised by this, he continued. "What are your names?" His question was met with silence once again. "Oh! You must be playing a game. Okay, I'll play!" Flurry sat there in silence for a moment – but like most children, he was unable to sit still for very long.

Flurry jumped back up to his feet and nudged the taller lion on the shoulder. "Do you want to play a different game?" The hunched over plush still would not answer or even look at Flurry.

Flurry felt disappointed in his new friends. In fact, he felt shunned. These new acquaintances did not seem to have any interest in being his friend. Flurry was filled with frustration. He crossed his arms and abruptly sat down beside them. In a bit of a tantrum, he said, "I wish you guys would talk to me. I just want to be friends." At that very moment, the taller of the two lions turned his head, looked right at Flurry, and waved to him.

Flurry's countenance instantly improved. He jumped to his feet. "Oh, yeah! You don't have a mouth. No wonder you didn't speak to me," Flurry reasoned out loud. Flurry then walked up to the second lion. To this little lion he asked, "What's your name?" The small fellow answered, "Well, I believe my name is Boaz. That's what my caretakers have called me. As for him ..." Boaz pointed at the taller lion, just over his right shoulder. "His name is Noah, but he won't be able to answer you, because he doesn't have a mouth."

"Nice to meet you, Boaz and Noah!"

The polar bear interjected, "My name is Caboose!"

"Hi, Caboose! I'm Flurry!"

"Oh! Hi! My name is Caboose!" the polar bear answered again.

"Uh … yeah, you already said that," Flurry replied uncertainly. He was a bit perplexed by Caboose's comment.

"I did? Oh, okay," Caboose replied.

During their interaction, the rabbit muttered to himself and hopped away, but the brown bunny came to a halt when Flurry obstructed his path. He glared at the teddy bear cub. Flurry reached down and patted the bunny on the head. "You're a cute little mouse. What's your name?"

The bunny pushed Flurry's paw from his head, turned around, and took off in the opposite direction. As he sped away, he muttered something that Flurry could not make out.

"His name is Honja. Or at least I think that's his name. That's what our parents call him," Boaz interjected.

"Oh! Hello, Honja! Nice to meet you!" Flurry hollered at him. Honja had hopped to the other side of the dresser's surface.

"Don't mind him. He can be really moody. He's probably angry that you thought he was a mouse. He's a bunny rabbit. Oh! He doesn't like being patted on the head either!" Boaz added. "Essentially, he likes to keep to himself."

"Oh! Sorry, Honja!" Flurry called out to the rabbit. He hoped his apology would patch up any hard feelings. "Why can't I understand what he's saying?" Flurry turned back toward Boaz for the answer.

"Well, our father purchased him in another country. So he doesn't speak our language. Luckily, he seems to be able to understand us," the lion cub replied.

"Oh! Well, I'm sure I can figure it out. I'm smart!" Flurry assured Boaz. Then Flurry stopped for a moment and pondered, *Was that also a vain thought? Oops!*

Now, unbeknownst to Flurry, he was actually responsible for the other four plush animals having been brought to life. Somehow, Christopher Kringle's act of having given life to Flurry left a residual effect on the cub. This was how Flurry sped up time when he wanted to go to the toy factory on his first day of work.

Being ignorant of this miraculous ability, Flurry had managed to create new friends for himself, though he assumed that these four plush animals had always had the ability to speak and move around just as he did. The bear cub was none the wiser that he had anything to do with it.

Needless to say, Flurry's new foster family was in for yet another surprise. The lady of the house was at her desk. She entered in grades for her students when, out of the corner of her eye, she saw something golden brown which stood at her door. She turned and beheld a tall slender lion that waved at her. She gasped and jumped up from her chair. "Noah?" she said. *This isn't possible*, she thought to herself.

She cautiously walked toward the lion just before he ran off toward the living room. As she reached the open door, a bunny rabbit ran past her, closely followed by a polar bear. She then heard a strange sound from behind. Startled, Lynn spun around and looked back at the computer. There she found Boaz, who typed away on her keyboard. "Hey! What are you doing?" she exclaimed and rushed over to the computer.

"I'm just looking at the computer, Mommy," the little lion answered.

Her mouth dropped open. She tried to take in and understand the events that unfolded right before her eyes. The house was in a state of chaos as they ran all over the place. Uncertainly she asked, "You can talk?"

"Of course I can!" Boaz replied.

"Yeah! Isn't it great, Mommy?" Flurry called to her from the doorway.

"Flurry! How did this happen? How's this even possible?" she shouted at the little bear cub.

He perceived that he was in some kind of trouble. Flurry quickly replied, "Caboose did it! Okay, goodbye!" Flurry tried to run off, but his mother was fast on her feet. The young lady grabbed his scarf before he could get away.

Flurry looked back at her, embarrassed. "Flurry!" she exclaimed. She expected an account from her bear cub.

"What are you talking about, Mommy? These are my friends," Flurry answered, unclear as to why his mother was so surprised by this.

She did not know what to say, so she released the little bear. Flurry rushed out of the room just as Noah had turned on the television. After a period of disbelief and shock, she got her senses back.

The lady left the room and entered the living area. She stood there and called out to the circus that ran around her house, "Noah! Boaz! Caboose! Honja! What are all of you doing?" They froze in their tracks and looked up at her.

"Playing?" they answered with a unified voice.

She rubbed her eyes and shook her head. "I can't believe this is happening," she softly whispered to herself before she addressed them again. "All of you, come here!" They all ran to her and lined up. "Flurry, too!" she added while Flurry attempted to sneak away.

Flurry quickly ran up and got in line. He held his arms behind his back, as he usually did when he was in trouble. "Yes, Mommy?"

"Flurry, did you do this?" she asked.

"Do what?" Flurry asked innocently.

"Bring them to life. Did you do that?" she inquired again.

Flurry was quite dumbfounded by her question. He did the best he could to answer her. "Mommy, they've always been alive. I just went into your room to talk to them, and we all decided to play together."

Their mother sighed and shook her head in disbelief. *How am I going to manage five of them now? Flurry's already a handful as it is*, she thought to herself. "Okay, there are some ground rules. Nobody is allowed to watch the television, play video games, or be on the computer without getting my permission first. Nobody is allowed to go outside without me or my husband's supervision; it isn't safe. Stay away from the stove and the oven, they're dangerous, and you can catch on fire."

They all listened closely as she continued through her rules. When she was finished, they resumed their festivities and played games together.

Later that evening, when her husband pulled into the driveway, she quickly rushed out the back door to debrief him on the situation. He had to be warned before she allowed him to enter the house. She was certain that he would have had the same reaction she had previously experienced – confusion and disbelief.

Instead of one child, they now had five furry boys to look after. The next day, their father got different materials together and built beds and nightstands for all of them. He and his wife decided to make the computer room a bedroom for their new family members. Their mother grew accustomed to lovingly referring to them collectively as "the fuzzies".

Flurry was quick to decorate his part of the room. He added a drawing of himself with his new parents. In addition to his drawing was a photograph of himself. He taped them both up on the pastel green wall next to his bed.

To his new parents' disapproval, he also wrote his name on the wall in crayon. They were very displeased with Flurry over this, but what was done was done. It was not the last time he would do something like that.

A dresser sat between Flurry and Noah's beds, and they each got one of the drawers to use as their own. The same was done for Caboose, Boaz, and Honja, though Boaz and Honja shared a drawer together.

One morning, Flurry woke up earlier than normal. He crawled out of bed and noticed that the other fuzzies were still asleep. His mother typed away at her computer. She was hard at work preparing for her class. The sun's rays beamed in through the window. Its light illuminated the grain pattern of the hardwood floor.

Flurry hopped down and put his bed back in order, as he was taught to do. Just as he pulled his blue, snowflake-covered bedspread up over his pillow, he looked around and realized how happy he was with his new life and family in Middleasia.

Flurry realized that his foster mother and father loved him and cared about him very much. He got to have visits from his teddy bear parents, he had new friends, and many new and exciting experiences. He thought about how he would never have met such great people or have had his new and wonderful friends if he were still in the wintery land of Mezarim. Flurry fondly recalled all of the new food that had been introduced to him, especially his favorites – spaghetti and chocolate milk. Flurry looked around, content, and with a smile on his face he thought to himself, *There's no place like home.*

From that day forward, Flurry had many wonderful and exciting experiences. Little did Flurry know that he was about to embark on a series of adventures that would challenge him in every way. The cub's mettle would be tested in the purifying fire of upcoming trials. Flurry was unaware that his decisions were about to affect the lives of everyone on his entire world. Flurry was special. Flurry's purpose was yet to be discovered. Whether he liked it or not, he had a destiny.

Some time passed. One lovely morning, golden rays beamed through Flurry's bedroom window. The melody of birds clearly …

*****

Nomi paused. She realized that some of the cubs listened intently, while others had dozed off. She glanced at Christopher. He nodded to acknowledge that it was late and she could stop reading.

"… the end." Nomi added, closed the book, and set it on her lap.

Suddenly, the cubs broke from their trance. They virtually all raised their paws at the same time.

The questions poured in like a flood.

"That's all?"

"That's not all!"

"You're only halfway!"

"Where's the rest?"

"Yeah, what about his adventures?"

"I saw him here recently! When did he get to come back?"

"How does he travel between worlds?"

"Why doesn't Noah speak?"

"Where was Vallidore?"

Christopher decided to quickly intervene. "Okay, okay! That's enough! It's late! All of you need to get some shut eye. We can read more about Flurry's adventures later."

"But! But!" said one cub.

"We want to know more!" whined many of the other bundles of fur.

"That story was only about where he came from. If you want to know about his adventures, come back next time. I'll save it for the next story time we have together," Christopher stated firmly.

"Awww," complained the teddy bear cubs as they gathered up their things.

The cubs could not wait until they could hear what remained of the story. They desperately wanted to hear about Flurry's first adventure in the land of the Sourpie. They had heard two different versions of that tale and maybe, just maybe, Mr. Kringle would set the record straight.

The night grew late, and the moon had risen high above the village. The streets were empty. The teddy bear cubs prepared for bed. Off in the distance a howl was heard. The land of Mezarim was not accustomed to the presence of wolves. The guardian elves kept close watch over the region to protect all who lived under Christopher's jurisdiction.

The villagers recognized the sound. They came out into the streets. Ursus prepared for some new visitors.

Christopher, Catherine, and Nomi also heard the howl. "Wait here. I'll go meet them and bring them here," Christopher insisted. "But first, I need to do something else." Christopher grabbed a metal door handle, walked into another room of the house, and closed the door behind him. He placed the door handle upon the wall and pulled down. The wall opened up to reveal a completely different room with a young, oriental lady who sat on a couch.

Meanwhile, Catherine prepared some

food for the new guests which were about to arrive.

Another howl sounded, followed by a third and a fourth. The cadence of many feet could be heard tromping through the snow. A pack of enormous wolves were headed straight toward Ursus. They were being led by a white wolf with blue markings on his fur. Some of the wolves carried passengers.

As the wolves came across the mountain, the white wolf stopped, and upon his back stood none other than Flurry himself. He looked back at his companions and shouted, "We're here!"

On the backs of other wolves were Noah, Caboose, Boaz, Honja, and a female teddy bear with cream-colored fur, a blue dress, and two little bows on her head – one above each ear.

Flurry had finally returned from a very long adventure that had kept him away for nearly three months. He was relieved to be back. With excitement upon his face, he looked out over the valley and pointed at Ursus. "Come on, Doggy! Let's go home!"

EPILOGUE
THE PROMISE

Lynn sat in her living room and read a book. It had been all that she could do to take her mind off of the events of the previous three months. The only thing that kept her going was the promise from a tall, bearded man. That very man now stood in her house. He lingered at the threshold of an open door which led back into his own home.

At that moment, that doorway bridged Flurry's world to her own. She had not expected such a sudden visit, but it was more than welcome. She had waited for this day long enough.

She instantly closed her book and stood up. Christopher smiled and looked at the young lady before he spoke. "I have good news. We've found him. He's back!"

*****

Eleven months prior, Mr. and Mrs. Snow sat in their empty home. They had received many visits from friends and family. Christopher himself stopped by frequently. However, life was not the same without their son.

Flurry had been in Middleasia for nearly a month now. Mr. and Mrs. Snow had been granted a visit, which greatly improved their countenance, but it was not enough.

The bears desperately longed for their son. The absence of his laughter made their house an empty husk of what it used to be. In fact, they even longed for his antics. Even his mischief was pined for.

Mrs. Snow stared out the window and watched the snowflakes fall. She was lost in deep reflection. She thought about how it seemed like only yesterday when she named her son after the little flakes that accumulated on the windowsill.

A tear formed in her eye. She would have cried, if her attention had not been taken away by the knock at her door. She wiped away the tear and approached the entryway.

She opened the door and found Christopher. He knelt down beside her door. He was too large to be invited in, but what intrigued the lady of the house the most was what Christopher held in his arms.

Mrs. Snow gasped. "Is that?" were the only words she could get out from her mouth. Christopher smiled and handed her a baby bear cub. Mrs. Snow cried. "Why? What's this for?"

"I know nothing can ever replace Flurry. That's not my intent. I just think this little cub might add some cheer to your life in the meantime," Christopher answered.

At that moment, Mr. Snow came down the steps. His wife turned and smiled at him, with tears that still streamed from her eyes. Mr. Snow's eyes filled with tears of his own. He approached his wife and peered down at the adorable baby bear.

Before Mr. Snow could say anything, Christopher stood up and walked away. Christopher had not strolled too far off before he called back, "I plan to invite Flurry back for a visit soon. Until then, make the most of your time with your new daughter."

ABOUT J.S. SKYE

J.S. Skye grew up in the Midwestern region of the United States. At a very young age, it was apparent that he was very talented. Finding that he was gifted in music and art, he plunged himself into both. As time passed, he set aside music to focus even more of his attention on developing his skills as an illustrator.

All throughout his years in school, J.S. Skye spent every available moment creating and developing fictional worlds. Caring about realism, he developed multiple people groups, countries, worlds, and even languages. His fictional realms were created through both written and visual mediums.

After traveling to almost a dozen different countries and studying different cultures, J.S. Skye decided to implement his interests in ancient cultures, history, languages, mythology, and more into his writings. He decided it was best to pour his heart and passion into writing instead of having divided interests between both art and literature.

J.S. Skye has accumulated a fairly large collection of his various writings. These stories range from all types of different genres such as mystery, science fiction, fantasy, and even horror. Friends encouraged the aspiring writer to produce a novel and see how things progressed from there.

J.S. Skye's first novel, *The Granted Wish*, was met with cheerful affirmation. The positive feedback was overwhelming and unexpected. Fans of his *Flurry the Bear* novels grew and began to clamor for more. From this point forward, his first novel series came to be.

For more information or to get in touch with J.S. Skye personally, he may be contacted by e-mail at:

JS-Skye@FlurryTheBear.com

ALSO BY J.S. SKYE

Flurry the Bear – The Land of the Sourpie

Flurry the Bear – The Throne of Frost

Flurry the Bear – The Book of Snow

Flurry the Bear – The Rising Tide

www.ingramcontent.com/pod-product-compliance
Lightning Source LLC
Chambersburg PA
CBHW030332180626
46810CB00003B/1331

9 780692 866740